Influential LGBTQ+ Works of the Nineteenth Century

Walt Whitman
Theodore Winthrop
Joseph Sheridan Le Fanu
Agnes Mary Frances Robinson
Oscar Wilde
Edward Carpenter

Dover Publications
Garden City, New York

DOVER THRIFT EDITIONS

General Editor: Susan L. Rattiner
Editor of This Volume: Michael Croland

Influential LGBTQ+ Works of the Nineteenth Century is a new work, first published by Dover Publications in 2026. Readers should be forewarned that the text contains racial and cultural references of the era in which it was written and may be deemed offensive by today's standards.

Library of Congress Cataloging-in-Publication Data

Names: Whitman, Walt, 1819–1892 author | Winthrop, Theodore, 1828–1861 author | Le Fanu, Joseph Sheridan, 1814–1873 author | Robinson, A. Mary F. (Agnes Mary Frances), 1857–1944 author | Wilde, Oscar, 1854–1900 author | Carpenter, Edward, 1844–1929 author
Title: Influential LGBTQ+ works of the nineteenth century / Walt Whitman, Theodore Winthrop, Joseph Sheridan Le Fanu, Agnes Mary Frances Robinson, Oscar Wilde and Edward Carpenter.
Description: Garden City, New York : Dover Publications, 2026. | Series: Dover thrift editions | Summary: "This Dover original anthology explores how six authors, including Walt Whitman and Oscar Wilde, represented the queer community during the nineteenth century. These works of prose and poetry offer valuable context for contemporary discussions about early LGBT+ advocacy"—Provided by publisher.
Identifiers: LCCN 2025019060 | ISBN 9780486855455 trade paperback
Subjects: LCSH: Sexual minorities' writings, American | Sexual minorities' writings, English | Literature, Modern—19th century | Sexual minorities in literature | Queer theory | LCGFT: Literature
Classification: LCC PS508.S49 I54 2026 | DDC 810.8/035266—dc23/eng/20250625
LC record available at https://lccn.loc.gov/2025019060

Printed in Canada
85545701 2025
www.doverpublications.com

Note

It would be a phenomenal undertaking to encapsulate all of the literary feats by queer authors and representation for the LGBTQ+ community during the nineteenth century, both implied and direct, in a single book. Many authors were willing to face scrutiny and risks to their personal safety in order to shed light on a marginalized community. This anthology is a curated selection of excerpts, most of which highlight the diverse array of sexual and gender identities with humanity and sensitivity.

Many scholars believe that Walt Whitman, an icon of American literature, was a member of the queer community, although he never made any public assertions about his sexual preferences. "Calamus," a group of poems that was a later addition to his larger collection *Leaves of Grass*, focuses on what Whitman refers to as the "manly love of comrades." Considered to have his most explicit references to male homoeroticism, *Leaves of Grass* was banned from libraries and schools and faced scrutiny from Whitman's contemporaries. In 1865, he was fired from his government job when his boss read a copy of the book. The backlash and censorship of *Leaves of Grass* parallels the experience of queer authors in the twenty-first century due to controversial book bans, which repress representation for the LGBTQ+ community.

Theodore Winthrop's *Cecil Dreeme* has risen in notoriety due to reprints by New York University Press and University of Pennsylvania Press in 2016. Both publishers called out the explicit queer themes at the heart of the relationship between the main characters. Cecil Dreeme—a woman living in disguise as a man who "comes out" to their close, intimate friend Robert Byng—illustrates the fluid transition between genders.

Carmilla was a prototype for the lesbian vampire trope that is still prevalent in modern queer horror romance novels. Joseph Sheridan Le Fanu did not shy away from the romantic attraction between Carmilla and Laura, as well as Carmilla's intimate preferences for only women. While there are debates about Le Fanu's intentions in creating a queer character, the two women are portrayed as mutually attracted to one another. Modern readers often embrace the relationship between Carmilla and Laura.

Agnes Mary Frances Robinson's romantic poetry in "Songs and Dreams" in *An Italian Garden: A Book of Songs* is lyrical, dreamy, and sometimes forlorn in its address of unnamed women. "A Ballad of Forgotten Tunes" is one of the few poems in this collection that names a specific person. Most literary scholars believe V.L.—who is also called Vernon—to be Vernon Lee, the pseudonym used by Robinson's friend and alleged lover, Violet Paget.

Oscar Wilde was well-known in nineteenth-century Britain for his extravagant character and his intimate relationships with other men. He was tried for and found guilty of gross indecency, a nineteenth-century term often used to persecute homosexuals. Prosecutors used *The Picture of Dorian Gray* as evidence of what they considered to be his immoral behavior. The novel features two male characters who admire and seek the attention of the titular Dorian Gray, who is proclaimed to be of striking beauty. This desire could be interpreted as lustful or romantic.

The anthology wraps up with a message from Edward Carpenter that echoes modern arguments against ideologies and laws that are rooted in homophobia and oppression. Authors, especially those who were early gay rights activists like Carpenter, have been making the same argument for centuries. Carpenter's work provides context for what gay rights activism looked like in time periods that are typically not associated with LGBTQ+ representation and activism. In *Homogenic Love and Its Place in a Free Society*, he shows that the fight for equality has been long and arduous but has been fought with an indefatigable group of people through protests, rallies, speeches, and literary representation.

These works haven't just had an impact on the visibility of the queer community. They have also had an impact on the literature we read today. Visibility is one of the strongest forms of activism for marginalized groups, especially in a medium as widespread as literature. Despite attempts to oppress their voices, modern queer authors follow in the footsteps of these earlier authors in their depictions of complex and empathetic same-sex relationships and characters that do not fall within strict gender conventions. We can celebrate the visibility these nineteenth-century authors, and many others, have provided for the modern queer community by aiding in the groundwork for validation within a heteronormative society.

Contents

"Calamus" from *Leaves of Grass*

Walt Whitman

IN PATHS UNTRODDEN

In paths untrodden,
In the growth by margins of pond-waters,
Escaped from the life that exhibits itself,
From all the standards hitherto publish'd, from the pleasures,
profits, conformities,
Which too long I was offering to feed my soul,
Clear to me now standards not yet publish'd, clear to me that my
soul,
That the soul of the man I speak for rejoices in comrades,
Here by myself away from the clank of the world,
Tallying and talk'd to here by tongues aromatic,
No longer abash'd, (for in this secluded spot I can respond as
I would not dare elsewhere,)
Strong upon me the life that does not exhibit itself, yet contains all
the rest,
Resolv'd to sing no songs to-day but those of manly attachment,
Projecting them along that substantial life,
Bequeathing hence types of athletic love,
Afternoon this delicious Ninth-month in my forty-first year,
I proceed for all who are or have been young men,
To tell the secret of my nights and days,
To celebrate the need of comrades.

FOR YOU O DEMOCRACY

Come, I will make the continent indissoluble,
I will make the most splendid race the sun ever shone upon,
I will make divine magnetic lands,
With the love of comrades,
With the life-long love of comrades.

I will plant companionship thick as trees along all the rivers of America, and along the shores of the great lakes, and all over the prairies,
I will make inseparable cities with their arms about each other's necks,
By the love of comrades,
By the manly love of comrades.

For you these from me, O Democracy, to serve you ma femme!
For you, for you I am trilling these songs.

THESE I SINGING IN SPRING

These I singing in spring collect for lovers,
(For who but I should understand lovers and all their sorrow and
joy?
And who but I should be the poet of comrades?)
Collecting I traverse the garden the world, but soon I pass the
gates,
Now along the pond-side, now wading in a little, fearing not the
wet,
Now by the post-and-rail fences where the old stones thrown
there, pick'd from the fields, have accumulated,
(Wild flowers and vines and weeds come up through the stones
and partly cover them, beyond these I pass,)
Far, far in the forest, or sauntering later in summer, before I think
where I go,
Solitary, smelling the earthy smell, stopping now and then in the
silence,
Alone I had thought, yet soon a troop gathers around me,
Some walk by my side and some behind, and some embrace my
arms or neck,
They the spirits of dear friends dead or alive, thicker they come, a
great crowd, and I in the middle,
Collecting, dispensing, singing, there I wander with them,
Plucking something for tokens, tossing toward whoever is near
me,
Here, lilac, with a branch of pine,
Here, out of my pocket, some moss which I pull'd off a live-oak
in Florida as it hung trailing down,
Here, some pinks and laurel leaves, and a handful of sage,
And here what I now draw from the water, wading in the pond-
side,

(O here I last saw him that tenderly loves me, and returns again never to separate from me,
And this, O this shall henceforth be the token of comrades, this calamus-root shall,
Interchange it youths with each other! let none render it back!)
And twigs of maple and a bunch of wild orange and chestnut,
And stems of currants and plum-blows, and the aromatic cedar,
These I compass'd around by a thick cloud of spirits,
Wandering, point to or touch as I pass, or throw them loosely from me,
Indicating to each one what he shall have, giving something to each;
But what I drew from the water by the pond-side, that I reserve,
I will give of it, but only to them that love as I myself am capable of loving.

OF THE TERRIBLE DOUBT OF APPEARANCES

Of the terrible doubt of appearances,
Of the uncertainty after all, that we may be deluded,
That may-be reliance and hope are but speculations after all,
That may-be identity beyond the grave is a beautiful fable only,
May-be the things I perceive, the animals, plants, men, hills,
shining and flowing waters,
The skies of day and night, colours, densities, forms, may-be these
are (as doubtless they are) only apparitions, and the real
something has yet to be known,
(How often they dart out of themselves as if to confound me and
mock me!
How often I think neither I know, nor any man knows, aught of
them,)
May-be seeming to me what they are (as doubtless they indeed but
seem) as from my present point of view, and might prove (as of
course they would) nought of what they appear, or nought
anyhow, from entirely changed points of view;
To me these and the like of these are curiously answer'd by my
lovers my dear friends,
When he in whom I love travels with me or sits a long while
holding me by the hand,
When the subtle air, the impalpable, the sense that words and
reason hold not, surround us and pervade us,
Then I am charged with untold and untellable wisdom, I am
silent, I require nothing further,
I cannot answer the question of appearances or that of identity
beyond the grave,
But I walk or sit indifferent, I am satisfied,
He ahold of my hand has completely satisfied me.

THE BASE OF ALL METAPHYSICS

And now gentlemen,
A word I give to remain in your memories and minds,
As base and finalè too for all metaphysics.

(So to the students the old professor,
At the close of his crowded course.)

Having studied the new and antique, the Greek and Germanic
 systems,
Kant having studied and stated, Fichte and Schelling and Hegel,
Stated the lore of Plato, and Socrates greater than Plato,
And greater than Socrates sought and stated, Christ divine having
 studied long,
I see reminiscent to-day those Greek and Germanic systems,
See the philosophies all, Christian churches and tenets see,
Yet underneath Socrates clearly see, and underneath Christ the
 divine I see,
The dear love of man for his comrade, the attraction of friend to
 friend,
Of the well-married husband and wife, of children and parents,
Of city for city and land for land.

RECORDERS AGES HENCE

Recorders ages hence,
Come, I will take you down underneath this impassive exterior,
I will tell you what to say of me,
Publish my name and hang up my picture as that of the tenderest lover,
The friend the lover's portrait, of whom his friend his lover was fondest,
Who was not proud of his songs, but of the measureless ocean of love within him, and freely pour'd it forth,
Who often walk'd lonesome walks thinking of his dear friends, his lovers,
Who pensive away from one he lov'd often lay sleepless and dissatisfied at night,
Who knew too well the sick, sick dread lest the one he lov'd might secretly be indifferent to him,
Whose happiest days were far away through fields, in woods, on hills, he and another wandering hand in hand, they twain apart from other men,
Who oft as he saunter'd the streets curved with his arm the shoulder of his friend, while the arm of his friend rested upon him also.

WHEN I HEARD AT THE CLOSE OF THE DAY

When I heard at the close of the day how my name had been receiv'd with plaudits in the capitol, still it was not a happy night for me that follow'd,
And else when I carous'd, or when my plans were accomplish'd, still I was not happy,
But the day when I rose at dawn from the bed of perfect health, refresh'd, singing, inhaling the ripe breath of autumn,
When I saw the full moon in the west grow pale and disappear in the morning light,
When I wander'd alone over the beach, and undressing bathed, laughing with the cool waters, and saw the sun rise,
And when I thought how my dear friend my lover was on his way coming, O then I was happy,
O then each breath tasted sweeter, and all that day my food nourish'd me more, and the beautiful day pass'd well,
And the next came with equal joy, and with the next at evening came my friend,
And that night while all was still I heard the waters roll slowly continually up the shores,
I heard the hissing rustle of the liquid and sands as directed to me whispering to congratulate me,
For the one I love most lay sleeping by me under the same cover in the cool night,
In the stillness in the autumn moonbeams his face was inclined toward me,
And his arm lay lightly around my breast—and that night I was happy.

ARE YOU THE NEW PERSON DRAWN TOWARD ME?

Are you the new person drawn toward me?
To begin with take warning, I am surely far different from what you suppose;
Do you suppose you will find in me your ideal?
Do you think it so easy to have me become your lover?
Do you think the friendship of me would be unalloy'd satisfaction?
Do you think I am trusty and faithful?
Do you see no further than this façade, this smooth and tolerant manner of me?
Do you suppose yourself advancing on real ground toward a real heroic man?
Have you no thought O dreamer that it may be all maya, illusion?

ROOTS AND LEAVES THEMSELVES ALONE

Roots and leaves themselves alone are these,
Scents brought to men and women from the wild woods and pond-side,
Breast-sorrel and pinks of love, fingers that wind around tighter than vines,
Gushes from the throats of birds hid in the foliage of trees as the sun is risen,
Breezes of land and love set from living shores to you on the living sea, to you, O sailors!
Frost-mellow'd berries and Third-month twigs offer'd fresh to young persons wandering out in the fields when the winter breaks up,
Love-buds put before you and within you whoever you are,
Buds to be unfolded on the old terms,
If you bring the warmth of the sun to them they will open and bring form, colour, perfume, to you,
If you become the aliment and the wet they will become flowers, fruits, tall branches and trees.

I SAW IN LOUISIANA A LIVE-OAK GROWING

I saw in Louisiana a live-oak growing,
All alone stood it and the moss hung down from the branches,
Without any companion it grew there uttering joyous leaves of dark green,
And its look, rude, unbending, lusty, made me think of myself,
But I wonder'd how it could utter joyous leaves standing alone there without its friend near, for I knew I could not,
And I broke off a twig with a certain number of leaves upon it, and twined around it a little moss,
And brought it away, and I have placed it in sight in my room,
It is not needed to remind me as of my own dear friends,
(For I believe lately I think of little else than of them,)
Yet it remains to me a curious token, it makes me think of manly love;
For all that, and though the live-oak glistens there in Louisiana solitary in a wide flat space,
Uttering joyous leaves all its life without a friend a lover near,
I know very well I could not.

TO A STRANGER

Passing stranger! you do not know how longingly I look upon
you,
You must be he I was seeking, or she I was seeking, (it comes to
me as of a dream,)
I have somewhere lived a life of joy with you,
All is recall'd as we flit by each other, fluid, affectionate, chaste,
matured,
You grew up with me, were a boy with me or a girl with me,
I ate with you and slept with you, your body has become not
yours only nor left my body mine only,
You give me the pleasure of your eyes, face, flesh, as we pass, you
take of my beard, breast, hands, in return,
I am not to speak to you, I am to think of you when I sit alone or
wake at night alone,
I am to wait, I do not doubt I am to meet you again,
I am to see to it that I do not lose you.

THIS MOMENT YEARNING AND THOUGHTFUL

This moment yearning and thoughtful sitting alone,
It seems to me there are other men in other lands yearning and thoughtful,
It seems to me I can look over and behold them in Germany, Italy, France, Spain,
Or far, far away, in China, or in Russia or Japan, talking other dialects,
And it seems to me if I could know those men I should become attached to them as I do to men in my own lands,
O I know we should be brethren and lovers,
I know I should be happy with them.

I HEAR IT WAS CHARGED AGAINST ME

I hear it was charged against me that I sought to destroy
institutions,
But really I am neither for nor against institutions,
(What indeed have I in common with them? or what with the
destruction of them?)
Only I will establish in the Mannahatta and in every city of these
States inland and seaboard,
And in the fields and woods, and above every keel little or large
that dents the water,
Without edifices or rules or any argument,
The institution of the dear love of comrades.

THE PRAIRIE-GRASS DIVIDING

The prairie-grass dividing, its special odour breathing,
I demand of it the spiritual corresponding,
Demand the most copious and close companionship of men,
Demand the blades to rise of words, acts, beings,
Those of the open atmosphere, coarse, sunlit, fresh, nutritious,
Those that go their own gait, erect, stepping with freedom and command, leading not following,
Those with a never-quell'd audacity, those with sweet and lusty flesh clear of taint,
Those that look carelessly in the faces of Presidents and governors, as to say *Who are you*?
Those of earth-born passion, simple, never constrain'd, never obedient,
Those of inland America.

WHEN I PERUSE THE CONQUER'D FAME

When I peruse the conquer'd fame of heroes and the victories of mighty generals, I do not envy the generals,
Nor the President in his Presidency, nor the rich in his great house,
But when I hear of the brotherhood of lovers, how it was with them,
How together through life, through dangers, odium, unchanging, long and long,
Through youth and through middle and old age, how unfaltering, how affectionate and faithful they were,
Then I am pensive—I hastily walk away filled with the bitterest envy.

NO LABOR-SAVING MACHINE

No labour-saving machine,
Nor discovery have I made,
Nor will I be able to leave behind me any wealthy bequest to
found a hospital or library,
Nor reminiscence of any deed of courage for America,
Nor literary success nor intellect, nor book for the book-shelf,
But a few carols vibrating through the air I leave,
For comrades and lovers.

A GLIMPSE

A glimpse through an interstice caught,
Of a crowd of workmen and drivers in a bar-room around the
stove late of a winter night, and I unremark'd seated in a
corner,
Of a youth who loves me and whom I love, silently approaching
and seating himself near, that he may hold me by the hand,
A long while amid the noises of coming and going, of drinking
and oath and smutty jest,
There we two, content, happy in being together, speaking little,
perhaps not a word.

WHAT THINK YOU I TAKE MY PEN IN HAND?

What think you I take my pen in hand to record?
The battle-ship, perfect-model'd, majestic, that I saw pass the offing to-day under full sail?
The splendours of the past day? or the splendour of the night that envelops me?
Or the vaunted glory and growth of the great city spread around me?—no;
But merely of two simple men I saw to-day on the pier in the midst of the crowd, parting the parting of dear friends,
The one to remain hung on the other's neck and passionately kiss'd him,
While the one to depart tightly prest the one to remain in his arms.

A LEAF FOR HAND IN HAND

A leaf for hand in hand;
You natural persons old and young!
You on the Mississippi and all the branches and bayous of the Mississippi!
You friendly boatmen and mechanics! you roughs!
You twain! and all processions moving along the streets!
I wish to infuse myself among you till I see it common for you to walk hand in hand.

I DREAM'D IN A DREAM

I dream'd in a dream I saw a city invincible to the attacks of the whole of the rest of the earth,
I dream'd that was the new city of Friends,
Nothing was greater there than the quality of robust love, it led the rest,
It was seen every hour in the actions of the men of that city,
And in all their looks and words.

SOMETIMES WITH ONE I LOVE

Sometimes with one I love I fill myself with rage for fear I effuse unreturn'd love,
But now I think there is no unreturn'd love, the pay is certain one way or another,
(I loved a certain person ardently and my love was not return'd,
Yet out of that I have written these songs.)

TO THE EAST AND TO THE WEST

To the East and to the West,
To the man of the Seaside State and of Pennsylvania,
To the Kanadian of the north, to the Southerner I love,
These with perfect trust to depict you as myself, the germs are in all men,
I believe the main purport of these States is to found a superb friendship, exaltè, previously unknown,
Because I perceive it waits, and has been always waiting, latent in all men.

FAST ANCHOR'D ETERNAL O LOVE!

Fast-anchor'd eternal O love! O woman I love!
O bride! O wife! more resistless than I can tell, the thought of you!
Then separate, as disembodied or another born,
Ethereal, the last athletic reality, my consolation,
I ascend, I float in the regions of your love O man,
O sharer of my roving life.

AMONG THE MULTITUDE

Among the men and women the multitude,
I perceive one picking me out by secret and divine signs,
Acknowledging none else, not parent, wife, husband, brother,
  child, any nearer than I am,
Some are baffled, but that one is not—that one knows me.
Ah lover and perfect equal,
I meant that you should discover me so by faint indirections,
And I when I meet you mean to discover you by the like in you.

O YOU WHOM I OFTEN AND SILENTLY COME

O you whom I often and silently come where you are that I may
  be with you,
As I walk by your side or sit near, or remain in the same room
  with you,
Little you know the subtle electric fire that for your sake is playing
  within me.

FULL OF LIFE NOW

Full of life now, compact, visible,
I, forty years old the eighty-third year of the States,
To one a century hence or any number of centuries hence,
To you yet unborn these, seeking you.

When you read these I that was visible am become invisible,
Now it is you, compact, visible, realising my poems, seeking me,
Fancying how happy you were if I could be with you and become
your comrade;
Be it as if I were with you. (Be not too certain but I am now with
you.)

THAT SHADOW MY LIKENESS

That shadow my likeness that goes to and fro seeking a livelihood,
chattering, chaffering,
How often I find myself standing and looking at it where it flits,
How often I question and doubt whether that is really me;
But among my lovers and carolling these songs,
O I never doubt whether that is really me.

Cecil Dreeme

Theodore Winthrop

CHAPTER XVIII.

ANOTHER CASSANDRA

Dreeme went on slowly and carefully with his work, after my closing remark of the last chapter. I continued to observe him for some moments in silence. His palette and brushes were kept with extreme neatness. The colors on the palette were arranged methodically, with an eye to artistic gradation; so that the darker of the smooth, oily drops squeezed from his paint-tubes made, as it were, a horizon of shadow on the outer rim of the palette. Within this little amphitheatre of hillocks, black, indigo, and brown, the dashes of brighter hue were disposed in concentric arcs, shading toward pure white at the focus. All his utensils and materials betokened the same orderliness and refinement; nothing was out of place, nothing daubed or soiled. So careful too was his handling, that he needed no over-sleeve to protect his own. The delicate hand and the flexible wrist seemed incapable of an awkward or a blundering motion. He could no more do a slovenly thing, than he could dance a break-down or smoke a pipe. This personal neatness was specially beautiful to me. In my laboratory, at my task of splitting atoms and unbraiding gases, I learnt from the exquisite order and proportion that Nature never forgets in her combinations to require the same of men. I found it in Dreeme. His genius in art was not of the ill-regulated, splashy, blotchy, boisterous class. Nothing coarse could come from those fine fingers.

"You elaborate your work with great care," said I, after some moments' silence, while the painter had been touching in dots of light, and then pausing, studying, and touching again, here a point and there a line.

"I *must* be careful and elaborate. It is partly the timidity of a novice. I feel that my hand lacks the precision of practice,—the rapid, unerring touch of a master. But besides, now, as my work approaches completion, I perceive a failure in creative power. I work feebly and painfully."

"Creative power of course is temporarily exhausted by a complete consistent creation. Jove felt empty-headed enough when he had thought Minerva into being. Lie fallow for a season, and your brain will teem again with images!"

"Yes, that is the law; but you must remember that my case is solitary. My picture is a spasm. It came to me prematurely, as a purpose and a power come in the paroxysms of a fever. I have spent all my large force in it."

"Your picture is older, subject and handling, than you, as I have said before. But music, painting, and poetry are gifts of the gods to the young."

"Older than my years? Ah yes!" he said, drearily. "I was in the immortal misery when I poured out my soul there. It was sore, sore, sore work. I pray that I may never need to create tragedy again. I pray that no new or ancient experience may compel me to confess and confide it to the impersonal world. No, I have wreaked my anguish, my pity, my shame for the guilty, on that canvas, and the virtue is gone out of me."

"Essay another vein! You have worked off bitterness. Open your heart to sweetness! In brighter mood, you will do fairer things without the tragic element."

"Since you and Locksley compelled me to accept the sweet gift of a life more hopeful, I have made some sketches in a less severe manner than my Lear. That was cruel tragedy. These are only anecdotes."

"Pray exhibit!"

"To so gentle a critic, I venture. Do not expect passion,—that I wished to spare myself. The sentiment is simple and commonplace enough."

He placed before me three sketchy pictures, able and rapid.

"You see," said he, "I play upon one idea or its reverse."

The first sketch depicted a young girl, caught in a snow-storm, and sunk, a mere shapeless thing, among the drifts in a dreary pinewood. A gentleman, in the costume of a Puritan soldier, stooped over her. Beside him stood a sturdy yeoman with a cloak and a basket. A few sunbeams cleft the pines, glinted on the hero's corslet, and warmed the group. It was a scene full of the pathos of doubtful hope.

"Thank you for my immortality," said I, "It was a pretty thought to put Locksley and myself in this scene of rescue,—me too in the steel and buff of that plucky old pioneer, the first Byng, with whose exploits I have bored you so often. I hope we were in time, before the maiden perished."

"The sunbeam seems to promise that," said he smiling, and handed me the next.

Second picture. Scene, the splendid salon of a French chateau. Through the window, a mad mob of *sans culottes* were visible, forcing the grand entrance. Within, myself—costume, purple velvet, lace, and rapier—and Locksley, in blouse and sabots, were bearing off a fainted lady, dark-haired, and robed in yellow.

"Twice immortal!" said I. "But why avert the heroine's face?"

"Good female models are hard to find. My heroine should be worthy of my hero. Have you one of your own, whose features I might insert?"

"Have I found my heroine? Not yet,—that is, not certainly."

Dreeme handed me the third picture. "My Incognita," said he, "is willing to encounter bad company out of gratitude to her benefactors. Please appreciate the compliment!"

Third picture. Scene, the same splendid salon of the same chateau. Without, instead of the *sans culottes,* a group of soldiers of the Republic stood on guard. Within, the same dark-haired lady,—costume, yellow satin (it reminded me of that coverlet of Louis Philippe's which had served Dreeme for wrapper),—the same heroine as in the second picture, sat with her back to the spectator. At a table beside her was an official personage, signing a passport. He was dressed with careful coxcombry in Robespierre's favorite color, and resembled that demon slightly, but enough to recall him. Behind him, I—yes, I myself again—could be seen through a half-opened closet-door, sullenly sheathing my sword in obedience to a sign from the lady. Locksley also was there, in blouse and stealthy bare feet, playing prudence to valor and holding me back.

"Ah!" said I, "another person with us in the pillory of your picture. Strange! Your Robespierre might almost be a portrait of Densdeth."

"Indeed! It is a typical bad face, and may resemble several bad men."

"Singularly like Densdeth!" I repeated. "The same cold-blooded resolve, the same latent sneer, the same suppressed triumph, even the coxcombry you have given to your gentle butcher of '93,—all are Densdeth's. May you not have seen and remembered his marked face?"

"Possibly." He evaded my inquiring look, as he replied.

"Perhaps he has stared at you for an instant in a crowd. Perhaps you have caught a look of his from the window of a railroad-car. He may at some moment, without your conscious notice, have stamped himself ineffaccably upon your mind."

"It may be. An artist's brain receives and stores images often without distinct volition. But you may lend my villain a likeness from your own memory."

"Yes; our talk about Densdeth, and your warnings against an exaggerated danger are fresh in my mind. Certainly, as I see the face, it is Densdeth's very self."

"Now," said Dreeme, "take your choice of my three sketches. Three simple stories,—which will you have? I painted them for your selection, and have taken much grateful pleasure in the work. One is for you, one for Locksley, one for myself,—a souvenir for each of us in happier days."

"Mine will be precious as a souvenir, apart from its great value as Art. And, let me tell you, Dreeme, in their manner, these studies are as able as your Lear. The anecdotes hold their own with the tragedy. I believe you are the man we have been waiting for."

"Your praise thrills me."

"Do not let it spoil you," said I, willing in my turn to act the Mentor.

"Mr. Byng," said he gravely, "my life has been so deepened and solemnized by earnest trial and bitter experience, that vanity is, I trust, annihilated. I shall do my work faithfully, because my nature commands me to it; but I can never have the exultant feeling of personal pride in it as mine."

"That too is a legitimate joy. You will have it when the world gives you its verdict, 'Well done.'"

Dreeme sighed, and seemed to shrink away.

"To face the world!" said he,—"how dare I? And yet I must. My scanty means will not last me many weeks longer."

"My dear Dreeme," said I, "my purse is not insolent with fulness; but it holds enough to keep two spiritual beings, like ourselves, in oysters and ale, slaw and 'Wing's pethy,'—crackers being thrown in."

"Thank you," said he, smiling; "but I suppose I must go out into daylight, brave my fate, and take my risk."

"There is no risk. You must succeed."

"Ah!" said he, and tears stood in his great sad eyes; "I speak of another risk. Of another danger, which I shudder at. Here I am safe, unharming and unharmed. How can I take up my life's responsibilities again?"

"Dreeme," said I, "in any other but you, I should almost say that these fancies were unmanly."

He evaded my eye, as I said this, but did not seem insulted.

"But," I continued, "there is a certain kind of courage in your working here alone,—enough to establish your character. If you want a rough pugilistic ally against this mysterious peril of yours, take me into your confidence. Here are my fists! they are yours. What ogre shall I hit? What dragon shall I choke?"

"You are neglecting my poor gift," said he, resolutely changing the subject; "make your choice of the three pictures, and I will show you my portfolio of drawings. You shall see what my fingers do when they obey the dictates of my careless fancy."

"I choose the third of the series. Neither of those where I or my semblance is the chief figure,—neither where I am doing, but where I am receiving the favor. My only regret is that I cannot look through the back of her head and see the features of the lady, whose gesture tells me, 'Sheathe sword and swallow ire!' Robespierre—Densdeth too, that adds to its value. I must hang it up where he can see it. I am curious to know whether he will recognize himself."

"O no! Promise me that you will not show it at present. No, not to any one!"

"What, not identify myself with the *début* of the coming man? May I not be your herald?"

"Wait, at least, till I am ready to follow up the announcement of my coming. No premature pæans, if you please!"

"I obey, of course. But I should vastly like to show it to Towers, Sion, and Pensal. You know I have a growing intimacy with that trio of great artists. They would heartily welcome your advent."

"Spare me the dread of their condemnation! Keep my little gift to yourself, at present! Here is my heap of drawings. Look at them, and judge with your usual kindness!"

"So these were the thoughts too hot for your brain to hold. These represent what you *must* say, not what you chose to say. I perceive that the bent of your mind is not toward tragedy."

Very masterly sketches they were! A fine fancy, a subtle imagination, a large heart, had conceived them, an accurate and severe artistic sense had controlled and developed the thought, and an unerring hand had executed it. Dreeme was a youth, certainly not more than twenty-one; and yet here was the maturity of complete manhood. Whether he had had opportunities for studying classic art, or whether his genius had seized in common life that fine quality which we name "classic," these drawings of his would have stood the test with the purest of the Italian masters, in the days before Italian art had suffered blight,—that blight which befell it when progress ceased in the land, and a tyrannical Church bade the nation pause and let the world go by.

Dreeme's female figures were not drawn with the liberal and almost riotous fancy of youth, which loves floating and flaunting draperies and a bold display of the nude. A chaster feeling had presided over the studies of this fine genius. There was a severe simplicity in his drawings of women. He seemed to have approached the purer sex with a loving reverence, never with that coarse freedom which debases the work of many able men, nullifying all spiritual beauty. One would say that the artist of these drawings had taken his mother and his sisters as models for the elevated and saintly beings, whom he had placed in scenes of calm beauty, and engaged in tender offices of mercy, pity, and pardon. I could safely name him Raphael-Angelico,—the title saves me longer criticism.

Strangely enough,—and here I recognized either a wound in Dreeme's life or a want in his character,—there was not one scene of love—that is, the love Cupid manages—in the collection. Not one scene where lovers, happy or hapless, figured. No pretty picture of consent and fondness. Not one of passion and fervor.

Now, a young man or a young maiden, in the early twenties, in whose mind love is not the primal thought, is a monstrosity, and must be studied and analyzed with a view to cure.

Either Dreeme's nature was still in the crude, green state, unripened by passion, or he had suffered so bitterly from some treachery in love that he could not reawaken the memory. Either he was ignorant of love's sweet torture, or he had felt the agony, without the healing touch.

I suspected the latter.

Often, recently, as my relations with Dreeme grew closer, I had been conscious of a peculiar jealous curiosity. I was now his nearest friend. But had he not had a nearer? If not in my sex, in the other? It was under the influence of this jealousy, that I said,—

"It seems almost an impertinence, Dreeme, to suggest a negative fault in this collection of admirable drawings; but I perceive a want. The subject of love,—the love that presses hands and kisses lips, the tender passion,—had you nothing to say of it?"

"No," said he, "I am too young."

"Bah! you are past twenty."

"Twenty-one—the very day of your coming."

"Too young! why, as for me, I was in love while my upper lip was only downy. The passion increased as that feature began to be districted off with hairs, stalwart, but sporadic. And ever since I have grown up to a real moustache, with ends that can be twirled, I have been in love, or just out and waiting to jump or tumble in again, the whole time."

"How is it now?"

"I hardly know. In love? or almost in? Which? In, I believe. I am tempted to offer you a confidence."

"I would rather not," said Dreeme, uneasily.

"O yes; you shall interpret my feelings. I admire a woman, whom it seems to me that I should love devotedly, if she were a little other than she is,—herself touched with a diviner delicacy,—her own sister self, a little angelized."

Dreeme evaded my questioning look, and made no reply. I paused a moment, while he painted a jewel, flashing on the white neck of his Goneril.

"Come," said I, "my Mentor, do not dodge responsibility! Your reply may affect my destiny."

He met my glance now, and replied, without hesitation, "Love that admits questions is no love."

"Perhaps I am suffering the penalty for the inconstant mood I have permitted myself heretofore. Perhaps I only want a steady and sincere purpose to love and trust, and I shall do so."

"Beware such perilous doubts!" said he earnestly. "With a generous character like yours, they lead to illusions. You will presently, out of self-reproach for at all doubting the woman you fancy, pass into a blind confidence, and so win some miserable shock, perhaps too late."

"Cassandra again! Cassandra in the other sex."

"Do not say Cassandra! that proves you intend to disdain my warning."

"Dear me! what solemn business we are making of my little flirtation!—a flirtation all on my side, by the way. In fact, I really believe I have cleared my head of my vague doubts of the unknown lady in question. They only needed to be put into words, in presence of a third party, to seem, as you say, utterly ungenerous."

"I am sorry that you forced the confidence upon me,—very sorry! But you would have it so."

"You talk as if you knew the lady, and considered her unfitted for me."

"Believe that I have discernment enough, knowing you, to know the class of woman who in this phase of your life will necessarily attract you. I can divine whom,—that is, what manner of person you will choose for a love, since you have characterized the man you are fascinated by as an intimate."

"Oh! you mean Densdeth."

"Yes; while you allow him to dominate you,—and mind, I take my impression from yourself,—you will naturally seek a counterpart of his in the other sex."

I grew ill at ease under this penetrating analysis of my secret feelings.

It was, of course, of Emma Denman that I had spoken.

Emma Denman was the woman I deemed myself on the verge of loving.

It was she whom I felt that I did not love, and yet ought to love. It was she whom I should have loved, without any shadow of hesitation, if she had been herself touched with a diviner feminineness, her own sister self, a thought more angelic.

I had sometimes had a painful lurking consciousness that if I were nobler than I was,—if my mind were more resolutely made up and unwavering on the side of virtue,—I should have applied the test of a higher and purer nature on my side to Emma Denman, and found her in some way fatally wanting. But whenever this injurious fancy stirred within me, I quelled it, saying, "If I were nobler, I should not have morbid notions about others. How can you learn to trust women while you allow yourself daily to listen, and only carelessly to protest, when Densdeth urges his doctrine, that women and men only wait opportunity to be base?"

In fact, in violation of an instinct, I was going through the process of resolving to love Emma Denman, because I distrusted her, and such vague distrust seemed an unchivalric disloyalty, a cruel wrong to a friend.

The strange coincidence of Dreeme's warning determined me to banish my superstitions. No more of this weakness! I would cultivate, or, as I persuaded myself, frankly yield to my passion for my childish flame, love her, and do my best to win her. I saw now how baseless were my doubts, when they came to be stated in words. Indeed, there was no name for one of these misty beings of the mind.

All this flashed across my mind as I continued mechanically turning over Dreeme's drawings. With the thought came the resolve. I would no more begrudge my faith. I would love Emma Denman, and by love make myself worthy of it.

> "The fleeting purpose never is o'ertook
> Unless the deed go with it,"

I half murmured to myself, and so, taking my leave of Dreeme for the morning, I passed to Denman's house.

From that time, I was the undeclared lover of Emma Denman, as I shall presently describe.

And you, Cecil Dreeme,—it was your warning that urged me so perversely to do violence to an unerring instinct.

How strangely and fatally we interfere, unconsciously, for one another's bliss or bale!

Churm away;

Densdeth my intimate;

Cecil Dreeme my friend of friends;

Emma Denman almost my love.

So matters stood with me and the other characters of this drama, two months from the day of my instalment in Chrysalis.

But let it not be understood that I had nothing to do except to study these few persons. My days were full, and often my nights, with hard and absorbing work I had undertaken in my profession. I touched the world on many sides. I came into collision with various characters. I had my daily life, like other men,—my real life, if you will, that handled substances, and did not deal in mysteries. This I am not describing. I am at pains to eliminate every fact and thought of mine which did not bear immediately upon the development of the story I here compel myself to write.

CHAPTER XIX.

CAN THIS BE LOVE?

MEANTIME MY INTIMACY with the Denmans had been growing closer.

With me Mr. Denman laid aside his usual manner, a mixture of reserve and uneasiness. He forgot his preoccupations, and talked with me frankly.

"If I had had a son, Byng," said he, "I could have wished him a young man like yourself. I suppose you will not quarrel with me if I expend a little fatherliness on you."

I was touched by this kindness. My distrust of him wore away. It is my nature to think gently and tenderly of others. I was in those relations with Mr. Denman where one sees the better side of character. I shared his liberal hospitality. I perceived that he did not love wealth for itself, but as power; and that he used this power often judiciously, always generously. The vanity of exercising power, the mistake of fancying himself a being of higher order than men of lesser influence, he seemed to have outgrown. And the power, with its duties attached, he often found a weary burden. I saw him a tired and saddened man, thankful for the freshening friendship of his junior. I gave him mine frankly.

Could such a man be called, as Churm had harshly called him, the murderer of his daughter? Surely not! I might believe him to have erred in that business; I could not deem him criminal. And, justifying him, I even did injustice to the memory of the dead Clara. Who knew what undiscovered or unpublished sorrowful motive she might not have had for a suicide? The dead have no friends to justify them.

But there was another reason for my favorable judgment on Mr. Denman. I loved, or thought I loved, or wished that I loved, his daughter.

Ever since my conversation with Cecil Dreeme, I had encouraged this passion. I had seen Emma Denman frequently, then constantly; it was now every day.

Her fascination grew in power. There was a certain effort in it; but what man disputes a woman's right to make effort to please him? With me her manner was anxious, and even agitated. Other men, now that the blackness of first mourning was past, began to be at the house. Them she treated with civil indifference, or indifferent cordiality, as they merited. With me she seemed always eagerly striving that I should not misapprehend her, always protesting against some possibility of a false impression.

Ah! now that I look back upon it all, how I pity her! No wonder that she grew thin and worn! No wonder that her gayety often struck me as forced or fantastic! When it did so seem, I said to myself that she was determined not to be crushed by that sad tragedy of her sister's death. I did not dream that her eager moods were tokens of the desperate struggle she was making against the inevitable tragedy of her own life.

Shall I go through all the history of the progress of my passion? Shall I say how, day by day, my sympathy for this motherless, sisterless girl deepened,—how I sorrowed for her that, amid all the splendor of her life, her heart was sad and empty, and so the life a vain show? how I, dreading what might be the fate of her father's wealth, pleased myself with the thought that, if disaster befell him, I could offer her the home and the heart of a hopeful working-man? Shall I re-edit such an old, old story, with the new illustrations drawn from my own experience?

I shrink from the task of opening an ancient wound.

I shrink, but yet I force myself to the anguish.

And time has changed that bygone grief into a lesson. I must write. No matter how dark, the story shall be told. Every man's precious or costly experience belongs to every brother-man. No man may be a miser of the sorrows by which he has bought the power to be strong, to be tender, to pardon the weak and the guilty. Perhaps by some warning I here utter I may persuade a young and hesitating soul to shudder back from the brink of sin. Often a timely trifle of a gentle word of admonition has struck a foully fair temptation dead. I know how the recurring fragrance of a flower that childhood loved, how the far-away sound of breakers on a beach where childhood wandered, how a weft of cloud, how the leap of a sunbeam, how the sudden jubilant carol of a bird, how a portrait of the pure Madonna on the wall, how a chance line on an open page,—how any such momentous trifle will save a wavering soul from a treachery or a crime,—will interpose an instant's check, and rescue the life from a remorse, guarding it for a repentance. Yes; whatever agony it costs me to revive this old history, I do now, after its lesson is fully thought out, of my sober judgment, revive it,—let who will murmur, "Bad taste!" let who will cry out, "Unhealthy!" let who will sigh, "Alas! have we not our own griefs? why burden us with yours?"

Did I, or not, love Emma Denman? Why could I not determine this question? I had my friends among men. Closest among these was Cecil Dreeme; his friendship I deemed more precious than the love of women. But among women, no other, none, was at all so charming to me as Emma.

She was to me far more beautiful than any beauty,—infinitely more beautiful, always, than any of those round, full, red beauties who are steadily supplied to the city market, overt or covert, for wives or mistresses to the men who pay money for either, and have nothing but money to give.

She was brilliant, frivolously brilliant perhaps; but we pardon a dash of frivolity in a young woman of fashion, all her life flattered and caressed, and untrained by daily contact with men of strong minds and women of strong hearts.

Emma Denman stood just on the hither brink of genius. It seemed that, if some magnificent emotion, some heart-opening joy or grief, could befall her, she would suddenly be promoted to become herself, and that self a genius. If she could be once in earnest, she would be a noble woman. Such a character has a mighty charm to a lover. He stirs himself with the thought that his love may give the awakening touch; that his passion may supply the ripening flame, and win the bud to bloom.

In music, in art, in thought, I felt that Emma Denman needed but one step to stand on the heights among the inspired. She seemed to feel this also, and to be always pleading tacitly with me to give her the slight aid she needed. She could not pass into the realms of the divine liberty of genius, for some gossamer wall, invisible to all but her, and against her strong as adamant.

I was terrified sometimes by her keenness of insight into bad motives, her comprehension of the labyrinthine causes of bad acts. It is a perilous knowledge. We must pay price for power. How had she bought this unerring perception of the laws of evil? How came she by this aged possession in her first youth?

How? I quelled my uneasiness with the thought that the sensitive touch of innocence is warned away from poisoned blossoms by the clammy airs that hang about them, and so recoils, and will not pluck the flower or gather the fruit. I said that the mere dread of evil will instruct a virgin soul where are those paths of evil it must shun. I said it is better to know sin and shun it, than to half ignore and half evade.

Since our first interview, our relations had grown more and more intimate without check. We named them brotherly and sisterly, as they had been in our childish days. She claimed the sister's privilege of presiding over my social life, and aiding me to make a choice in love.

Miss Denman led me about the grand round of society. She took me to see the belles for beauty, the belles for money, the belles for wit, the belles for magnetism, the belles for blood. And all of them she drew out to show their most attractive side, in fact, their better and more genuine nature. She persuaded each to reveal that the belle had not addled the woman.

And then she wondered that she could not persuade me to fall in love with one of these ladies.

I could not, of course, if only because her process made her appear superior to them all. I admired the kindliness with which she strove to put sparkle into the stupid girls, to dignify the trifling, to refine the vulgar,—and the teacher was to me an infinitely finer being than her scholars ever could become.

And so I told her,—but never yet with the words of a lover.

And so she insisted I should not think,—not craftily and with systematic coquetry. No, poor child! Ah, no! I acquit her of all such slight wiles and surface hypocrisy. But how could I know that she was sincerely striving to save us both from the tragedy of a mutual love?

And did I love her? The question implied a doubt, where there should be only undoubting conviction and compelling impulse.

Why doubt, Robert Byng?

There was surely no other affection in my heart that I was playing false. Surely none. My heart was free from any love of woman.

And my doubt was based upon a suspicion.

A suspicion! of what?

If I at all stated to myself, however faintly, what, it seemed to me such disloyalty that I despised myself for entertaining the unwholesome thought.

"You are not fit," I said, "for the society of a pure woman! Densdeth has spoilt you."

Thus I trained my affection the more tenderly for its weakness. Thus, ignorant and rejecting the sure law of nature, I strove to create the uncreatable, to construct what should have come into being and grown strong without interference, even without consciousness of mine. Thus I began to deem the sentiment I was manufacturing out of ruth and a loyal intention, as genuine, heart-felt love.

Bitter error! And to be punished bitterly!

CHAPTER XX.
A NOCTURNE

NIGHT! NIGHT IN the great city!

Night! when the sun, the eye of God, leaves men to their own devices; when the moon is so faint, and the stars so far away in the infinite, that their inspection and record are forgotten; when Light, the lawgiver and orderer of human life, withdraws, and mankind are free to break or obey the commands daylight has taught them.

Night! when the gas-lights, relit, reawaken harmful purposes, that had slept through all the hours of honest sunshine in their lairs; when the tigers and tigresses take their stand where their prey will be sure to come; when the rustic in the peaceful country, with leaves whispering and crickets singing around him, sees a glow on the distant horizon, and wonders if the bad city beneath it be indeed abandoned of its godly men, and burning for its crimes. Night! the day of the base, the guilty, and the desolate!

Every evening, when it was possible, of that late winter and wintry spring, I abandoned club, parlor, and ball-room, and all the attractions of the brilliant world, to wander with Cecil Dreeme about the gas-lit city, and study the side it showed to night. And yet the phenomena of vice and crime, my companion refused to consider fit objects of curiosity. Vice and crime were tacitly avoided by us. Dreeme's nature repelled even the thought of them. I was happy to know one solitary man whose mind the consciousness of evil could not make less virgin.

It chanced one evening, a fortnight after our conversation when Dreeme gave me the picture, that walking as usual, and quite late, we passed the Opera-House. Some star people were giving an extra performance on an off night. The last act of an heroic opera was just beginning. Dreeme hummed the final air,—a noble burst of triumph over a victory bought by a martyrdom.

"Your song makes me hungry to hear more," said I.

"I have been almost starving for music," he rejoined.

"Come in, then. You can take your stand in the lobby, with your mysterious cloak about you, and slouched hat over your eyes. I defy your best friend or worst foe to know you."

"No, no!" said he, nervously; "in the glare of a theatre I should excite suspicion. I should be seen."

"And pounced upon and hurried off to durance vile?" said I, lightly enough; for I began at last to fancy that his panic of concealment was the sole disorder of a singularly healthy brain. "Well, I will not urge it. I cannot spare you. I am selfish. I should soon go to the bad without my friend and Mentor."

"It is strange," said Dreeme, bitterly, "that I, with a soul white as daylight, should be compelled to lurk about like a guilty thing,—to be as one dead and buried."

"I thank the mystery that secludes you for my benefit, Dreeme," I said. "I dread the time when you will find a thousand friends, and many closer than I."

He dropped his cloak and took my arm. It was the first time he had given me this slight token of intimacy. We had been very distant in our personal intercourse. I am not a man to slap another on the back, shake him by the shoulder, punch him in the ribs, or indulge in any rude play or coarse liberties. Yet there is a certain familiarity among men, by which we, after our roughish and unbeautiful fashion, mean as much tenderness for our friends as women do by their sweet embraces and caresses. Nothing of this kind had ever passed between Dreeme and me. His reserve and self-dependence had made me feel that it would be an impertinence to offer even that kind of bodily protection which a bigger man holds ready for a lesser and slighter.

It surprised me, then, a little, when Dreeme, for the first time, took my arm familiarly.

"You have been a kind friend to me, Mr. Byng," said he; "there are not many men in the world who would have treated my retirement with such delicate forbearance and good faith."

"Do not give me too much credit. I have been a selfish friend. I know that I am a facile person, something of the chameleon; I need the fairer colors in contact with me to keep me from becoming an ugly brown reptile. Having this adaptability of character, I have had very close relations with many of the best and noblest; but of all the men I have ever known, your society charms me most penetratingly.

All the poetry in my nature being latent, I need precisely you to bring it to the surface. The feminine element is largely developed in you, as a poetic artist. It precisely supplies the want which a sisterless and motherless man, like myself, has always felt. Your influence over me is inexpressibly bland and soothing. You certainly are my good spirit. I like you so much, that I have been quite content with your isolation; I get you all to myself. These walks with you, since that famous oyster supper, the very day of my return home, have been the chief feature of my life. I count my hour with you as the pay for my scuffle with the world. A third party would spoil the whole! What would become of our confidence, our intimate exchange of thought on every possible subject, if there were another fellow by, who might be a vulgarian or a muff? What could we do with a chap to whom we should have to explain our metaphysics, give page and line for our quotations, interpret our puns, translate our allusions, analyze our intuitions, define our God? Such a companion would take the sparkle and the flash of this rapid and unerring sympathy out of our lives. No, Dreeme, this isolation of yours suits me; and since you continue to tolerate my society, I must suit you. We form a capital exclusive pair, close as any of the historic ones,—Orestes and Pylades, for example,—to close my long discourse classically."

"Do not compare us to those ill-omened two. Orestes was ordained to slay his parent for her sin," my friend rejoined, in an uneasy tone.

"It was a judicial murder,—the guiltless execution of a decree of fate. And all turned out happily at last, you remember. Orestes became king of Argos, and gave his sister in marriage to his Pylades, the faithful. Who knows but when your tragic duty is over, whatever it be, and you have brought the guilty to justice, you will resume your proper crown, and find a sister for me, your Pylades, the faithful? If my present flame should not smile, that would be admirable. Your sister for me would make our brotherhood actual."

"My sister for you!" said Dreeme, with an accent almost of horror; and I could feel, by his arm in mine, that a strong shudder ran through him.

We had by this time passed from the side-front of the Opera-House, where this conversation began, had walked along Quatorze Street, and turned up into the Avenue. Quatorze Street, as only a total stranger need be informed, is named in triumphant remembrance of the minikin monarch whom we defeated in the old French war. The crossing of Quatorze Street and the Avenue was, at that time, the very focus of fashion. Within half a mile of that corner, Everybody lived—Everybody who was not Nobody.

It was mid-March. Lent was in full sigh. Balls were over until Easter. Fasting people cannot take violent exercise. One can dance on full, but not on meagre diet,—on turkey, not on fish. But in default of balls, Mrs. Bilkes, still a leader of fashion, had her Lent evenings. They were The Thing, so Everybody agreed, and this evening was one of them. I had deserted for my walk with Dreeme.

Mrs. Bilkes's house was just far enough above Quatorze Street, on the Avenue, to be in the van of the upward march of fashion. Files of carriages announced that all the world was with her that evening. The usual band discoursed the usual music within; but wanting the cadence of dancers' feet to enliven them, those Lenten strains came dolefully forth.

We were passing this mansion when Dreeme had last spoken. Before I had time to ask him what meant his agitation at the thought of me for possible brother-in-law, the factotum of the Bilkes party, the well-known professional, hailed me from the steps, where he stood in authority; for by the bright light from the house he could easily recognize me.

"What, Mr. Byng! You wont drop in upon us? They're packed close as coffins inside, but there's always room for another like yourself. Better come in,—Mrs. Bilkes will take on tremendous if she finds I let you go by without stopping."

I paused a moment, half disgusted, half amused by the privileged man's speech. As I did so, a gentleman coming down the steps addressed me. And it is such trivial pauses as these that bid us halt till Destiny overtakes our unconscious steps.

I turned with a slight start, for I had not observed the new-comer as an acquaintance until he was at my side.

It was Densdeth.

He looked, with his keen, hasty glance, at my companion. He seemed to recognize him as a stranger. He did not bow, but turned to me, and said,—

"What, Byng! Are you not going in? It is very brilliant. All the fair penitents are there, keeping Lent, in their usual severe simplicity of penitential garb. I asked Matilda Mildood if I should give her a bit of partridge and some chicken-salad. 'I'm quite ashamed of you, Mr. Densdeth,' says Matilda, with the air of one resolutely mortifying the flesh; 'don't you remember it's Lent. Oysters and lobster-salad, if you please, and a little terrapin, if there is any.' "

While Densdeth made this talk, he glanced again at my companion. Dreeme had withdrawn his arm, and stood a little apart, half turned away from us, avoiding notice, as usual.

"Don't throw away your cigar, Byng," continued Densdeth, taking out his case, and stepping toward the lamp-post, to make, as it seemed to me, a very elaborate selection. "Give me a light first. Will you try one of mine?"

"No, thank you. I have had my allowance."

Densdeth took my cigar to light his. The slight glow was sufficient to illuminate his face darkly. Its expression seemed to me singularly cruel and relentless. It was withal scornful and triumphant. Something evidently had happened which gave Densdeth satisfacton. Whom had he vanquished to-night?

The cigar would not draw.

"Bah!" said Densdeth, tearing it in two, with his white-gloved hands, with a manner of dainty torture, as if he were inflicting an indignity upon a foe. "Bah!" said he, taking out another cigar, with even more elaborate selection, and as he did so glancing, quick and sharp, at my friend, who had retreated from the lamp. "I don't allow cigars, any more than other creatures, to baffle me. Excuse me, Byng, for detaining you. The second trial must succeed; if not, I'll try a third time,—*that* always wins. Thanks!"

He lighted his cigar. Again by the glow I observed the same relentless, triumphant look.

Densdeth turned down the Avenue. I rejoined Dreeme. He took my arm again and clung to it almost weakly.

"What is the matter, Dreeme?" I asked, my tenderness for him all awake.

No answer, but a nervous pressure on my arm.

"You are tired. Shall we turn back?"

"Not the way that man has gone," said he.

"Why not? What do you fear?"

"I heard him name himself Densdeth. I saw his face—that cruel face of his. Mr. Byng,—my dear friend, Robert Byng,—that man is evil to the core. You call me your Mentor, your good influence; take my warning! Obey me, and shun him, as you would a fiend. You say that I have a fresh nature; believe that my instinct of aversion for a villain is unerring."

"Is not this prejudice?" said I, somewhat moved by his panic, but still fancying so much alarm idle.

"It might before have been prejudice, derived from your own account of him; but now I have seen him, face to face."

"A glance merely, and in a dusky light."

"Yes, but one look at that face of his sears it into the heart."

"You seem to have been as inquisitive about him as he about you. He studied your back pretty thoroughly. In fact, I believe it was to observe you that he made such parade of breaking up his delinquent cigar. He evidently meant to know for what comrade I was abandoning the charms of the Bilkes *soirée*."

"I shudder at the thought of such a man's observation. What ugly fate brought me here?"

Dreeme turned, and looked back.

I involuntarily did the same.

The Avenue, at that late hour, was nearly deserted of promenaders. As far away as two blocks behind us, I noticed the spark of a cigar, and as the smoker passed a gas-light, I could see him take the cigar from his lips with a white-gloved hand. He even seemed to brandish it triumphantly.

"He is following us!" cried Dreeme.

The painter whirled me about a corner, and dragged me, almost at a run, along several humbler streets. At last we turned into one of the avenues by the North River, far away from the beat of any guest of Mrs. Bilkes.

There Dreeme paused, and spoke.

"Good exercise I have given you by my panic," said he, with a forced laugh. "How absurd I have been! Pardon me! You are aware how nervous I get, being so much shut up alone. And then, you know, I was only hurrying you away from your devil."

"Strange fellow you are, Dreeme! I suppose this very strangeness is one element of your control over me. You excite my curiosity in degree, though not in kind, quite as much as Densdeth does. And now that you and he are brought together, I hope these two mysterious personages will explain each other by some flash of hostile electricity. I wait for light from the meeting of the thunder-clouds."

"It must be very late," said Dreeme in a weary tone. "What a dismal part of the city! This squalor sickens me. These rows of grog-shops infect me with utter hopelessness. Sin—sin everywhere, and the sorrow that never can be divorced from sin! How can we escape? How can we save others? These nocturnal wanderings of ours have told me of a breadth and a depth of misery that years of a charitable lifetime would never have revealed. If I ever have opportunities for action and influence, I shall know my duty, and how to do it. I see, Mr. Byng, as I have before told you, that you do not thoroughly share my sympathy for poverty and suffering and crime."

"Perhaps not fully. My heart is not so tender as yours. I cannot seem to make other people's distress my personal business, as you do. I endure the misfortunes of strangers with reasonable philosophy. Suffering, like pain, I suppose is to be borne heroically, until it passes off. Every man has his hard times."

"You are not cruel," said Dreeme, "but you talk cruelly on a subject you hardly understand. Wait until the hours of your own bitterness come, and you will learn the precious lesson of sympathy! You will soften to others, and most to those who suffer for no fault of theirs,—the wronged, driven to despair by wrong-doing in those they love,—the erring, visited with what we name ruin, for some miserable mistake of inexperience. But let us hasten home! I have never felt so sick at heart, so doubtful of the future, so oppressed by the 'weary weight of all this unintelligible world,' as I do at this moment."

"Dreeme, are you never to take your future into your own hands, and live a healthy, natural life, like other men? Think of yourself! Do not be so wretched with other people's faults! You cannot annihilate the troubles that have made you unhappy; but do not brood over them. Be young, and live young, in sunshine and gayety."

"Be young!" said he, more drearily than ever.

"Yes; make me your confidant! Face down your difficulties! If you do not trust my experience, and think me too recent in the country to give you practical help, there is my friend, Mr. Churm. He will be here to-morrow from a journey. Churm is true as steel. Trust him! He and I will pull you through."

"I trust no one but you. Do not press me yet. I am generally contented, as you know, with my art and your society. Only to-night the sight of that bad man has discomposed me."

"Discomposed is a mild term," said I, as I unlocked the outer door of Chrysalis.

"Well, I am composed now. But I wish," said he in a trepidating way, that belied his words, "that you would see me safe to my door."

I did so, and we parted, closer friends than ever.

Densdeth, Cecil Dreeme, Emma Denman,—these three figures battled strangely in my dreams.

Carmilla

Joseph Sheridan Le Fanu

CHAPTER III.

WE COMPARE NOTES

WE FOLLOWED THE *cortège* with our eyes until it was swiftly lost to sight in the misty wood; and the very sound of the hoofs and wheels died away in the silent night air.

Nothing remained to assure us that the adventure had not been an illusion of a moment but the young lady, who just at that moment opened her eyes. I could not see, for her face was turned from me, but she raised her head, evidently looking about her, and I heard a very sweet voice ask complainingly, "Where is mamma?"

Our good Madame Perrodon answered tenderly, and added some comfortable assurances.

I then heard her ask:

"Where am I? What is this place?" and after that she said, "I don't see the carriage; and Matska, where is she?"

Madame answered all her questions in so far as she understood them; and gradually the young lady remembered how the mis-adventure came about, and was glad to hear that no one in, or in attendance on, the carriage was hurt; and on learning that her mamma had left her here, till her return in about three months, she wept.

I was going to add my consolations to those of Madame Perrodon when Mademoiselle de Lafontaine placed her hand upon my arm, saying:

"Don't approach, one at a time is as much as she can at present converse with; a very little excitement would possibly overpower her now."

As soon as she is comfortably in bed, I thought, I will run up to her room and see her.

My father in the meantime had sent a servant on horseback for the physician, who lived about two leagues away; and a bedroom was being prepared for the young lady's reception.

The stranger now rose, and leaning on Madame's arm, walked slowly over the drawbridge and into the castle gate.

In the hall, servants waited to receive her, and she was conducted forthwith to her room.

The room we usually sat in as our drawing-room is long, having four windows, that looked over the moat and drawbridge, upon the forest scene I have just described.

It is furnished in old carved oak, with large carved cabinets, and the chairs are cushioned with crimson Utrecht velvet. The walls are covered with tapestry, and surrounded with great gold frames, the figures being as large as life, in ancient and very curious costume, and the subjects represented are hunting, hawking, and generally festive. It is not too stately to be extremely comfortable; and here we had our tea, for with his usual patriotic leanings he insisted that the national beverage should make its appearance regularly with our coffee and chocolate.

We sat here this night, and with candles lighted, were talking over the adventure of the evening.

Madame Perrodon and Mademoiselle De Lafontaine were both of our party. The young stranger had hardly lain down in her bed when she sank into a deep sleep; and those ladies had left her in the care of a servant.

"How do you like our guest?" I asked, as soon as Madame entered. "Tell me all about her?"

"I like her extremely," answered Madame, "she is, I almost think, the prettiest creature I ever saw; about your age, and so gentle and nice."

"She is absolutely beautiful," threw in Mademoiselle, who had peeped for a moment into the stranger's room.

"And such a sweet voice!" added Madame Perrodon.

"Did you remark a woman in the carriage, after it was set up again, who did not get out," inquired Mademoiselle, "but only looked from the window?"

No, we had not seen her.

Then she described a hideous black woman, with a sort of coloured turban on her head, who was gazing all the time from the carriage window, nodding and grinning derisively towards the ladies, with gleaming eyes and large white eye-balls, and her teeth set as if in fury.

"Did you remark what an ill-looking pack of men the servants were?" asked Madame.

"Yes," said my father, who had just come in, "ugly, hang-dog looking fellows, as ever I beheld in my life. I hope they mayn't rob the poor lady in the forest. They are clever rogues, however; they got everything to rights in a minute."

"I dare say they are worn out with too long travelling," said Madame. "Besides looking wicked, their faces were so strangely lean, and dark, and sullen. I am very curious, I own; but I dare say the young lady will tell us all about it to-morrow, if she is sufficiently recovered."

"I don't think she will," said my father, with a mysterious smile, and a little nod of his head, as if he knew more about it than he cared to tell us.

This made me all the more inquisitive as to what had passed between him and the lady in the black velvet, in the brief but earnest interview that had immediately preceded her departure.

We were scarcely alone, when I entreated him to tell me. He did not need much pressing.

"There is no particular reason why I should not tell you. She expressed a reluctance to trouble us with the care of her daughter, saying she was in delicate health, and nervous, but not subject to any kind of seizure—she volunteered that—nor to any illusion; being, in fact, perfectly sane."

"How very odd to say all that!" I interpolated. "It was so unnecessary."

"At all events it *was* said," he laughed, "and as you wish to know all that passed, which was indeed very little, I tell you. She then said, 'I am making a long journey of *vital* importance'—she emphasized the word—'rapid and secret; I shall return for my child in three months; in the meantime, she will be silent as to who we are, whence we come, and whither we are travelling.' That is all she said. She spoke very pure French. When she said the word 'secret,' she paused for a few seconds, looking sternly, her eyes fixed on mine. I fancy she makes a great point of that. You saw how quickly she was gone. I hope I have not done a very foolish thing, in taking charge of the young lady."

For my part, I was delighted. I was longing to see and talk to her; and only waiting till the doctor should give me leave. You, who live in towns, can have no idea how great an event the introduction of a new friend is, in such a solitude as surrounded us.

The doctor did not arrive till nearly one o'clock; but I could no more have gone to my bed and slept, than I could have overtaken, on foot, the carriage in which the princess in black velvet had driven away.

When the physician came down to the drawing-room, it was to report very favourably upon his patient. She was now sitting up, her pulse quite regular, apparently perfectly well. She had sustained no injury, and the little shock to her nerves had passed away quite harmlessly. There could be no harm certainly in my seeing her, if we both wished it; and with this permission, I sent, forthwith, to know whether she would allow me to visit her for a few minutes in her room.

The servant returned immediately to say that she desired nothing more.

You may be sure I was not long in availing myself of this permission.

Our visitor lay in one of the handsomest rooms in the schloss. It was, perhaps, a little stately. There was a sombre piece of tapestry opposite the foot of the bed, representing Cleopatra with the asps to her bosom; and other solemn classic scenes were displayed, a little faded, upon the other walls. But there was gold carving, and rich and varied colour enough in the other decorations of the room, to more than redeem the gloom of the old tapestry.

There were candles at the bed side. She was sitting up; her slender pretty figure enveloped in the soft silk dressing-gown, embroidered with flowers, and lined with thick quilted silk, which her mother had thrown over her feet as she lay upon the ground.

What was it that, as I reached the bed side and had just begun my little greeting, struck me dumb in a moment, and made me recoil a step or two from before her? I will tell you.

I saw the very face which had visited me in my childhood at night, which remained so fixed in my memory, and on which I had for so many years so often ruminated with horror, when no one suspected of what I was thinking.

It was pretty, even beautiful; and when I first beheld it, wore the same melancholy expression.

But this almost instantly lighted into a strange fixed smile of recognition.

There was a silence of fully a minute, and then at length *she* spoke; *I* could not.

"How wonderful!" she exclaimed. "Twelve years ago, I saw your face in a dream, and it has haunted me ever since."

"Wonderful indeed!" I repeated, overcoming with an effort the horror that had for a time suspended my utterances. "Twelve years ago, in vision or reality, *I* certainly saw you. I could not forget your face. It has remained before my eyes ever since."

Her smile had softened. Whatever I had fancied strange in it, was gone, and it and her dimpling cheeks were now delightfully pretty and intelligent.

I felt reassured, and continued more in the vein which hospitality indicated, to bid her welcome, and to tell her how much pleasure her accidental arrival had given us all, and especially what a happiness it was to me.

I took her hand as I spoke. I was a little shy, as lonely people are, but the situation made me eloquent, and even bold. She pressed my hand, she laid hers upon it, and her eyes glowed, as, looking hastily into mine, she smiled again, and blushed.

She answered my welcome very prettily. I sat down beside her, still wondering; and she said:

"I must tell you my vision about you; it is so very strange that you and I should have had, each of the other, so vivid a dream, that each should have seen, I you and you me, looking as we do now, when of course we both were mere children. I was a child, about six years old, and I awoke from a confused and troubled dream, and found myself in a room, unlike my nursery, wainscoted clumsily in some dark wood, and with cupboards and bedsteads, and chairs and benches placed about it. The beds were, I thought, all empty, and the room itself without any one but myself in it; and I, after looking about me for some time, and admiring especially an iron candlestick, with two branches, which I should certainly know again, crept under one of the beds to reach the window; but as I got from under the bed, I heard some one crying; and looking up, while I was still upon my knees, I saw *you*—most assuredly you—as I see you now; a beautiful young lady, with golden hair and large blue eyes, and lips—your lips—you, as you are here. Your looks won me; I climbed on the bed and put my arms about you, and I think we both fell asleep. I was aroused by a scream; you were sitting up screaming. I was frightened, and slipped down upon the ground, and, it seemed to me, lost consciousness for a moment; and when I came to myself, I was again in my nursery at home. Your face I have never forgotten since. I could not be misled by mere resemblance. You *are* the lady whom I then saw."

It was now my turn to relate my corresponding vision, which I did, to the undisguised wonder of my new acquaintance.

"I don't know which should be most afraid of the other," she said, again smiling. "If you were less pretty I think I should be very much afraid of you, but being as you are, and you and I both so young, I feel only that I have made your acquaintance twelve years ago, and have already a right to your intimacy; at all events, it does seem as if we were destined, from our earliest childhood, to be friends. I wonder whether you feel as strangely drawn towards me as I do to you; I have never had a friend—shall I find one now?" She sighed, and her fine dark eyes gazed passionately on me.

Now the truth is, I felt rather unaccountably towards the beautiful stranger. I did feel, as she said, "drawn towards her," but there was also something of repulsion. In this ambiguous feeling, however, the sense of attraction immensely prevailed. She interested and won me; she was so beautiful and so indescribably engaging.

I perceived now something of languor and exhaustion stealing over her, and hastened to bid her good night.

"The doctor thinks," I added, "that you ought to have a maid to sit up with you to-night; one of ours is waiting, and you will find her a very useful and quiet creature."

"How kind of you, but I could not sleep, I never could with an attendant in the room. I shan't require any assistance—and, shall I confess my weakness, I am haunted with a terror of robbers. Our house was robbed once, and two servants murdered, so I always lock my door. It has become a habit—and you look so kind I know you will forgive me. I see there is a key in the lock."

She held me close in her pretty arms for a moment and whispered in my ear, "Good-night, darling, it is very hard to part with you, but good-night; to-morrow, but not early, I shall see you again."

She sank back on the pillow with a sigh, and her fine eyes followed me with a fond and melancholy gaze, and she murmured again, "Good-night, dear friend."

Young people like, and even love, on impulse. I was flattered by the evident, though as yet undeserved, fondness she showed me. I liked the confidence with which she at once received me. She was determined that we should be very dear friends.

Next day came and we met again. I was delighted with my companion; that is to say, in many respects.

Her looks lost nothing in daylight—she was certainly the most beautiful creature I had ever seen, and the unpleasant remembrance of the face presented in my early dream, had lost the effect of the first unexpected recognition.

She confessed that she had experienced a similar shock on seeing me, and precisely the same faint antipathy that had mingled with my admiration of her. We now laughed together over our momentary horrors.

CHAPTER IV.

HER HABITS—A SAUNTER

I TOLD YOU that I was charmed with her in most particulars.

There were some that did not please me so well.

She was above the middle height of women. I shall begin by describing her. She was slender, and wonderfully graceful. Except that her movements were languid—*very* languid—indeed, there was nothing in her appearance to indicate an invalid. Her complexion was rich and brilliant; her features were small and beautifully formed; her eyes large, dark, and lustrous; her hair was quite wonderful, I never saw hair so magnificently thick and long when it was down about her shoulders; I have often placed my hands under it, and laughed with wonder at its weight. It was exquisitely fine and soft, and in colour a rich very dark brown, with something of gold. I loved to let it down, tumbling with its own weight, as, in her room, she lay back in her chair talking in her sweet low voice, I used to fold and braid it, and spread it out and play with it. Heavens! If I had but known all!

I said there were particulars which did not please me. I have told you that her confidence won me the first night I saw her; but I found that she exercised with respect to herself, her mother, her history, everything in fact connected with her life, plans, and people, an ever-wakeful reserve. I dare say I was unreasonable, perhaps I was wrong; I dare say I ought to have respected the solemn injunction laid upon my father by the stately lady in black velvet. But curiosity is a restless and unscrupulous passion, and no one girl can endure, with patience, that hers should be baffled by another. What harm could it do anyone to tell me what I so ardently desired to know? Had she no trust in my good sense or honour? Why would she not believe me when I assured her, so solemnly, that

I would not divulge one syllable of what she told me to any mortal breathing?

There was a coldness, it seemed to me, beyond her years, in her smiling melancholy persistent refusal to afford me the least ray of light.

I cannot say we quarrelled upon this point, for she would not quarrel upon any. It was, of course, very unfair of me to press her, very ill-bred, but I really could not help it; and I might just as well have let it alone.

What she did tell me amounted, in my unconscionable estimation—to nothing.

It was all summed up in three very vague disclosures:

First.—Her name was Carmilla.

Second.—Her family was very ancient and noble.

Third.—Her home lay in the direction of the west.

She would not tell me the name of her family, nor their armorial bearings, nor the name of their estate, nor even that of the country they lived in.

You are not to suppose that I worried her incessantly on these subjects. I watched opportunity, and rather insinuated than urged my inquiries. Once or twice, indeed, I did attack her more directly. But no matter what my tactics, utter failure was invariably the result. Reproaches and caresses were all lost upon her. But I must add this, that her evasion was conducted with so pretty a melancholy and deprecation, with so many, and even passionate declarations of her liking for me, and trust in my honour, and with so many promises that I should at last know all, that I could not find it in my heart long to be offended with her.

She used to place her pretty arms about my neck, draw me to her, and laying her cheek to mine, murmur with her lips near my ear, "Dearest, your little heart is wounded; think me not cruel because I obey the irresistible law of my strength and weakness; if your dear heart is wounded, my wild heart bleeds with yours. In the rapture of my enormous humiliation I live in your warm life, and you shall die—die, sweetly die—into mine. I cannot help it; as I draw near to you, you, in your turn, will draw near to others, and learn the rapture of that cruelty, which yet is love; so, for a while, seek to know no more of me and mine, but trust me with all your loving spirit."

And when she had spoken such a rhapsody, she would press me more closely in her trembling embrace, and her lips in soft kisses gently glow upon my cheek.

Her agitations and her language were unintelligible to me.

From these foolish embraces, which were not of very frequent occurrence, I must allow, I used to wish to extricate myself; but my energies seemed to fail me. Her murmured words sounded like a lullaby in my ear, and soothed my resistance into a trance, from which I only seemed to recover myself when she withdrew her arms.

In these mysterious moods I did not like her. I experienced a strange tumultuous excitement that was pleasurable, ever and anon, mingled with a vague sense of fear and disgust. I had no distinct thoughts about her while such scenes lasted, but I was conscious of a love growing into adoration, and also of abhorrence. This I know is paradox, but I can make no other attempt to explain the feeling.

I now write, after an interval of more than ten years, with a trembling hand, with a confused and horrible recollection of certain occurrences and situations, in the ordeal through which I was unconsciously passing; though with a vivid and very sharp remembrance of the main current of my story. But, I suspect, in all lives there are certain emotional scenes, those in which our passions have been most wildly and terribly roused, that are of all others the most vaguely and dimly remembered.

Sometimes after an hour of apathy, my strange and beautiful companion would take my hand and hold it with a fond pressure, renewed again and again; blushing softly, gazing in my face with languid and burning eyes, and breathing so fast that her dress rose and fell with the tumultuous respiration. It was like the ardour of a lover; it embarrassed me; it was hateful and yet overpowering; and with gloating eyes she drew me to her, and her hot lips travelled along my cheek in kisses; and she would whisper, almost in sobs, "You are mine, you *shall* be mine, and you and I are one for ever." Then she has thrown herself back in her chair, with her small hands over her eyes, leaving me trembling.

"Are we related," I used to ask; "what can you mean by all this? I remind you perhaps of some one whom you love; but you must not, I hate it; I don't know you—I don't know myself when you look so and talk so."

She used to sigh at my vehemence, then turn away and drop my hand.

Respecting these very extraordinary manifestations I strove in vain to form any satisfactory theory—I could not refer them to affectation or trick. It was unmistakably the momentary breaking out of suppressed instinct and emotion. Was she, notwithstanding her mother's volunteered denial, subject to brief visitations of insanity; or was there here a disguise and a romance? I had read in old story books of such things. What if a boyish lover had found his way into the house, and sought to prosecute his suit in masquerade, with the assistance of a clever old adventuress? But there were many things against this hypothesis, highly interesting as it was to my vanity.

I could boast of no little attentions such as masculine gallantry delights to offer. Between these passionate moments there were long intervals of common-place, of gaiety, of brooding melancholy, during which, except that I detected her eyes so full of melancholy fire, following me, at times I might have been as nothing to her. Except in these brief periods of mysterious excitement her ways were girlish; and there was always a languor about her, quite incompatible with a masculine system in a state of health.

In some respects her habits were odd. Perhaps not so singular in the opinion of a town lady like you, as they appeared to us rustic people. She used to come down very late, generally not till one o'clock, she would then take a cup of chocolate, but eat nothing; we then went out for a walk, which was a mere saunter, and she seemed, almost immediately, exhausted, and either returned to the schloss or sat on one of the benches that were placed, here and there, among the trees. This was a bodily languor in which her mind did not sympathise. She was always an animated talker, and very intelligent.

She sometimes alluded for a moment to her own home, or mentioned an adventure or situation, or an early recollection, which indicated a people of strange manners, and described customs of which we knew nothing. I gathered from these chance hints that her native country was much more remote than I had at first fancied.

As we sat thus one afternoon under the trees a funeral passed us by. It was that of a pretty young girl, whom I had often seen, the daughter of one of the rangers of the forest. The poor man was walking behind the coffin of his darling; she was his only child, and he looked quite heartbroken. Peasants walking two-and-two came behind, they were singing a funeral hymn.

I rose to mark my respect as they passed, and joined in the hymn they were very sweetly singing.

My companion shook me a little roughly, and I turned surprised.

She said brusquely, "Don't you perceive how discordant that is?"

"I think it very sweet, on the contrary," I answered, vexed at the interruption, and very uncomfortable, lest the people who composed the little procession should observe and resent what was passing.

I resumed, therefore, instantly, and was again interrupted. "You pierce my ears," said Carmilla, almost angrily, and stopping her ears with her tiny fingers. "Besides, how can you tell that your religion and mine are the same; your forms wound me, and I hate funerals. What a fuss! Why, *you* must die—*everyone* must die; and all are happier when they do. Come home."

"My father has gone on with the clergyman to the churchyard. I thought you knew she was to be buried to-day."

"*She*? I don't trouble my head about peasants. I don't know who she is," answered Carmilla, with a flash from her fine eyes.

"She is the poor girl who fancied she saw a ghost a fortnight ago, and has been dying ever since, till yesterday, when she expired."

"Tell me nothing about ghosts. I shan't sleep to-night if you do."

"I hope there is no plague or fever coming; all this looks very like it," I continued. "The swineherd's young wife died only a week ago, and she thought something seized her by the throat as she lay in her bed, and nearly strangled her. Papa says such horrible fancies do accompany some forms of fever. She was quite well the day before. She sank afterwards, and died before a week."

"Well, *her* funeral is over, I hope, and *her* hymn sung; and our ears shan't be tortured with that discord and jargon. It has made me nervous. Sit down here, beside me; sit close; hold my hand; press it hard—hard—harder."

We had moved a little back, and had come to another seat.

She sat down. Her face underwent a change that alarmed and even terrified me for a moment. It darkened, and became horribly livid; her teeth and hands were clenched, and she frowned and compressed her lips, while she stared down upon the ground at her feet, and trembled all over with a continued shudder as irrepressible as ague. All her energies seemed strained to suppress a fit, with which she was then breathlessly tugging; and at length a low convulsive cry of suffering broke from her, and gradually the hysteria subsided. "There! That comes of strangling people with hymns!" she said at last. "Hold me, hold me still. It is passing away."

And so gradually it did; and perhaps to dissipate the sombre impression which the spectacle had left upon me, she became unusually animated and chatty; and so we got home.

This was the first time I had seen her exhibit any definable symptoms of that delicacy of health which her mother had spoken of. It was the first time, also, I had seen her exhibit anything like temper.

Both passed away like a summer cloud; and never but once afterwards did I witness on her part a momentary sign of anger. I will tell you how it happened.

She and I were looking out of one of the long drawing-room windows, when there entered the court-yard, over the drawbridge, a figure of a wanderer whom I knew very well. He used to visit the schloss generally twice a year.

It was the figure of a hunchback, with the sharp lean features that generally accompany deformity. He wore a pointed black beard, and he was smiling from ear to ear, showing his white fangs. He was dressed in buff, black, and scarlet, and crossed with more straps and belts than I could count, from which hung all manner of things. Behind, he carried a magic-lantern, and two boxes, which I well knew, in one of which was a salamander, and in the other a mandrake. These monsters used to make my father laugh. They were compounded of parts of monkeys, parrots, squirrels, fish, and hedgehogs, dried and stitched together with great neatness and startling effect. He had a fiddle, a box of conjuring apparatus, a pair of foils and masks attached to his belt, several other mysterious cases dangling about him, and a black staff with copper ferrules in his hand. His companion was a rough spare dog, that followed at his heels, but stopped short, suspiciously at the drawbridge, and in a little while began to howl dismally.

In the meantime, the mountebank, standing in the midst of the court-yard, raised his grotesque hat, and made us a very ceremonious bow, paying his compliments very volubly in execrable French, and German not much better. Then, disengaging his fiddle, he began to scrape a lively air, to which he sang with a merry discord, dancing with ludicrous airs and activity, that made me laugh, in spite of the dog's howling.

Then he advanced to the window with many smiles and salutations, and his hat in his left hand, his fiddle under his arm, and with a fluency that never took breath, he gabbled a long advertisement of all his accomplishments, and the resources of the various arts which he placed at our service, and the curiosities and entertainments which it was in his power, at our bidding to display.

"Will your ladyships be pleased to buy an amulet against the oupire, which is going like the wolf, I hear, through these woods," he said, dropping his hat on the pavement. "They are dying of it right and left, and here is a charm that never fails; only pinned to the pillow, and you may laugh in his face."

These charms consisted of oblong slips of vellum, with cabalistic ciphers and diagrams upon them.

Carmilla instantly purchased one, and so did I.

He was looking up, and we were smiling down upon him, amused; at least, I could answer for myself. His piercing black eye, as he looked up in our faces, seemed to detect something that fixed for a moment his curiosity.

In an instant he unrolled a leather case, full of all manner of odd little steel instruments.

"See here, my lady," he said, displaying it, and addressing me, "I profess, among other things less useful, the art of dentistry. Plague take the dog!" he interpolated. "Silence, beast! He howls so that your ladyships can scarcely hear a word. Your noble friend, the young lady at your right, has the sharpest tooth—long, thin, pointed, like an awl, like a needle; ha, ha! With my sharp and long sight, as I look up, I have seen it distinctly; now if it happens to hurt the young lady, and I think it must, here am I, here are my file, my punch, my nippers; I will make it round and blunt, if her ladyship pleases; no longer the tooth of a fish, but of a beautiful young lady as she is. Hey? Is the young lady displeased? Have I been too bold? Have I offended her?"

The young lady, indeed, looked very angry as she drew back from the window.

"How dares that mountebank insult us so? Where is your father? I shall demand redress from him. My father would have had the wretch tied up to the pump, and flogged with a cart-whip, and burnt to the bones with the castle brand!"

She retired from the window a step or two, and sat down, and had hardly lost sight of the offender, when her wrath subsided as suddenly as it had risen, and she gradually recovered her usual tone, and seemed to forget the little hunchback and his follies.

My father was out of spirits that evening. On coming in he told us that there had been another case very similar to the two fatal ones which had lately occurred. The sister of a young peasant on his estate, only a mile away, was very ill, had been, as she described it, attacked very nearly in the same way, and was now slowly but steadily sinking.

"All this," said my father, "is strictly referable to natural causes. These poor people infect one another with their superstitions, and so repeat in imagination the images of terror that have infested their neighbours."

"But that very circumstance frightens one horribly," said Carmilla.

"How so?" inquired my father.

"I am so afraid of fancying I see such things; I think it would be as bad as reality."

"We are in God's hands; nothing can happen without His permission, and all will end well for those who love Him. He is our faithful creator; He has made us all, and will take care of us."

"Creator! *Nature!*" said the young lady in answer to my gentle father. "And this disease that invades the country is natural. Nature. All things proceed from Nature—don't they? All things in the heaven, in the earth, and under the earth, act and live as Nature ordains? I think so."

"The doctor said he would come here to-day," said my father, after a silence. "I want to know what he thinks about it, and what he thinks we had better do."

"Doctors never did me any good," said Carmilla.

"Then you have been ill?" I asked.

"More ill than ever you were," she answered.

"Long ago?"

"Yes, a long time. I suffered from this very illness; but I forget all but my pain and weakness, and they were not so bad as are suffered in other diseases."

"You were very young then?"

"I dare say; let us talk no more of it. You would not wound a friend?" She looked languidly in my eyes, and passed her arm round my waist lovingly, and led me out of the room. My father was busy over some papers near the window.

"Why does your papa like to frighten us?" said the pretty girl, with a sigh and a little shudder.

"He doesn't, dear Carmilla, it is the very furthest thing from his mind."

"Are you afraid, dearest?"

"I should be very much if I fancied there was any real danger of my being attacked as those poor people were."

"You are afraid to die?"

"Yes, everyone is."

"But to die as lovers may—to die together, so that they may live together. Girls are caterpillars while they live in the world, to be finally butterflies when the summer comes; but in the meantime there are grubs and larvae, don't you see—each with their peculiar propensities, necessities and structure. So says Monsieur Buffon, in his big book, in the next room."

Later in the day the doctor came, and was closeted with papa for some time. He was a skilful man, of sixty and upwards, he wore powder, and shaved his pale face smooth as a pumpkin. He and papa emerged from the room together, and I heard papa laugh, and say as they came out:

"Well, I do wonder at a wise man like you. What do you say to hippogriffs and dragons?"

The doctor was smiling, and made answer, shaking his head—

"Nevertheless, life and death are mysterious states, and we know little of the resources of either."

And so they walked on, and I heard no more. I did not then know what the doctor had been broaching, but I think I guess it now.

CHAPTER V.

A WONDERFUL LIKENESS

THIS EVENING THERE arrived from Gratz the grave, dark-faced son of the picture-cleaner, with a horse and cart laden with two large packing-cases, having many pictures in each. It was a journey of ten leagues, and whenever a messenger arrived at the schloss from our little capital of Gratz, we used to crowd about him in the hall, to hear the news.

This arrival created in our secluded quarters quite a sensation. The cases remained in the hall, and the messenger was taken charge of by the servants till he had eaten his supper. Then with assistants, and armed with hammer, ripping chisel, and turnscrew, he met us in the hall, where we had assembled to witness the unpacking of the cases.

Carmilla sat looking listlessly on, while one after the other the old pictures, nearly all portraits, which had undergone the process of renovation, were brought to light. My mother was of an old Hungarian family, and most of these pictures, which were about to be restored to their places, had come to us through her.

My father had a list in his hand, from which he read, as the artist rummaged out the corresponding numbers. I don't know that the pictures were very good, but they were, undoubtedly, very old, and some of them very curious also. They had, for the most part, the merit of being now seen by me, I may say, for the first time; for the smoke and dust of time had all but obliterated them.

"There is a picture that I have not seen yet," said my father. "In one corner, at the top of it, is the name, as well as I could read, 'Marcia Karnstein,' and the date '1698'; and I am curious to see how it has turned out."

I remembered it; it was a small picture, about a foot and a half high, and nearly square, without a frame; but it was so blackened by age that I could not make it out.

The artist now produced it, with evident pride. It was quite beautiful; it was startling; it seemed to live. It was the effigy of Carmilla!

"Carmilla, dear, here is an absolute miracle. Here you are, living, smiling, ready to speak, in this picture. Isn't it beautiful, papa? And see, even the mole on her throat."

My father laughed, and said, "Certainly it is a wonderful likeness," but he looked away, and to my surprise seemed but little struck by it, and went on talking to the picture-cleaner, who was also something of an artist, and discoursed with intelligence about the portraits or other works, which his art had just brought into light and colour, while *I* was more and more lost in wonder the more I looked at the picture.

"Will you let me hang this picture in my room, papa?" I asked.

"Certainly, dear," said he, smiling, "I'm very glad you think it so like. It must be prettier even than I thought it, if it is."

The young lady did not acknowledge this pretty speech, did not seem to hear it. She was leaning back in her seat, her fine eyes under their long lashes gazing on me in contemplation, and she smiled in a kind of rapture.

"And now you can read quite plainly the name that is written in the corner. It is not Marcia; it looks as if it was done in gold. The name is Mircalla, Countess Karnstein, and this is a little coronet over it, and underneath A. D. 1698. I am descended from the Karnsteins; that is, mamma was."

"Ah!" said the lady, languidly, "so am I, I think, a very long descent, very ancient. Are there any Karnsteins living now?"

"None who bear the name, I believe. The family were ruined, I believe, in some civil wars, long ago but the ruins of the castle are only about three miles away."

"How interesting!" she said, languidly. "But see what beautiful moonlight!" She glanced through the hall door, which stood a little open. "Suppose you take a little ramble round the court, and look down at the road and river."

"It is so like the night you came to us," I said.

She sighed, smiling.

She rose, and each with her arm about the other's waist, we walked out upon the pavement.

In silence, slowly we walked down to the drawbridge, where the beautiful landscape opened before us.

"And so you were thinking of the night I came here?" she almost whispered. "Are you glad I came?"

"Delighted, dear Carmilla," I answered.

"And you ask for a picture you think like me, to hang in your room," she murmured with a sigh, as she drew her arm closer about my waist, and let her pretty head sink upon my shoulder.

"How romantic you are, Carmilla," I said. "Whenever you tell me your story, it will be made up chiefly of some one great romance."

She kissed me silently.

"I am sure, Carmilla, you have been in love; that there is, at this moment, an affair of the heart going on."

"I have been in love with no one, and never shall," she whispered, "unless it should be you."

How beautiful she looked in the moonlight!

Shy and strange was the look with which she quickly hid her face in my neck and hair, with tumultuous sighs, that seemed almost to sob, and pressed in mine a hand that trembled.

Her soft cheek was glowing against mine. "Darling, darling," she murmured, "I live in you; and you would die for me, I love you so."

I started from her.

She was gazing on me with eyes from which all fire, all meaning had flown, and a face colourless and apathetic.

"Is there a chill in the air, dear?" she said drowsily. "I almost shiver; have I been dreaming? Let us come in. Come, come; come in."

"You look ill, Carmilla; a little faint. You certainly must take some wine," I said.

"Yes, I will. I'm better now. I shall be quite well in a few minutes. Yes, do give me a little wine," answered Carmilla, as we approached the door. "Let us look again for a moment; it is the last time, perhaps, I shall see the moonlight with you."

"How do you feel now, dear Carmilla? Are you really better?" I asked.

I was beginning to take alarm, lest she should have been stricken with the strange epidemic that they said had invaded the country about us.

"Papa would be grieved beyond measure," I added, "if he thought you were ever so little ill, without immediately letting us know. We have a very skilful doctor near this, the physician who was with papa to-day."

"I'm sure he is. I know how kind you all are: but, dear child, I am quite well again. There is nothing ever wrong with me, but a little weakness. People say I am languid; I am incapable of exertion; I can scarcely walk as far as a child of three years old; and every now and then the little strength I have falters, and I become as you have just seen me. But after all I am very easily set up again; in a moment I am perfectly myself. See how I have recovered."

So, indeed, she had; and she and I talked a great deal, and very animated she was; and the remainder of that evening passed without any recurrence of what I called her infatuations. I mean her crazy talk and looks, which embarrassed, and even frightened me.

But there occurred that night an event which gave my thoughts quite a new turn, and seemed to startle even Carmilla's languid nature into momentary energy.

"Songs and Dreams" from *An Italian Garden*

Agnes Mary Frances Robinson

TUSCAN MAY-DAY

The village girls have gone away
  To sing at every shrine,
The whole day long they sing and pray
  To Mary, maid divine.

I know so well the way they go,
  The very turn they took,
And all the chants they sing I know,
  And every Virgin's look:

Yet should I sing with them, and stand
  Before the Poor in heart,
Would she not reach her holy hand
  To thrust me out apart?

Beside the glimmering sea I sit,
  And watch the darkness fall;
The thirsty sand drinks up in it
  My tears, and hides them all.

The nearing voices swell and soar:
   Ave Mary! hark! Ave Mary!
Before the shrine upon the shore,
   The tired singers tarry.

I sang beside them at the spring,
   And in the weedy furrow;
But here I feel I dare not sing,
"Mary, Mary, Mary, Mother Mary,"
   My heart is mad with sorrow!

LOVE WITHOUT WINGS

EIGHT SONGS.

I.

I thought: no more the worst endures!
  I die, I end the strife,—
You swiftly took my hands in yours
  And drew me back to life!

II.

We sat when shadows darken,
  And let the shadows be;
Each was a soul to hearken,
  Devoid of eyes to see.

You came at dusk to find me;
  I knew you well enough . . .
O Lights that dazzle and blind me—
  It is no friend, but Love!

III.

How is it possible
  You should forget me,
Leave me for ever
  And never regret me!

I was the soul of you,
   Past Love or Loathing,
Lost in the whole of you . . .
   Now, am I nothing?

IV.

The fallen oak still keeps its yellow leaves
   But all its growth is o'er!
So, at your name, my heart still beats and grieves,
   Although I love no more.

V.

And so I shall meet you
   Again, my dear
How shall I greet you?
   What shall I hear?

I, you forgot!
   (But who shall say
You loved me not
   Yesterday?)

VI.

Ah me, do you remember still
   The garden where we strolled together,
The empty groves, the little hill
   Starred o'er with pale Italian heather?

And you to me said never a word,
   Nor I a single word to you,
And yet how sweet a thing was heard,
   Resolved, abandoned, by us two!

VII.

I know you love me not . . . I do not love you;
  Only at dead of night
I smile a little, softly dreaming of you
  Until the dawn is bright.

I love you not; you love me not; I know it!
  But when the day is long
I haunt you like the magic of a poet,
  And charm you like a song.

VIII.

O Death of things that are, Eternity
  Of things that seem;
Of all the happy past remains to me,
  To-day, a dream!

Long blessèd days of love and wakening thought,
  All, all are dead;
Nothing endures we did, nothing we wrought,
  Nothing we said.

But once I dreamed I sat and sang with you
  On Ida hill.
There, in the echoes of my life, we two
  Are singing still.

SEMITONES

I.

Give me a rose not merely sweet and fresh,
  Not only red and bright,
But caught about in such a thorny mesh
  As rankles in delight.

Smile on me, Sweet; but look not only kind
  The smile that most endears
Trembles on pallid lips from eyes half-blind
  With brine of bitter tears.

II.

Ah, could I clasp thee in mine arms,
  And thou not feel me there,
Asleep and free from vain alarms,
  Asleep and unaware!

Ah, could I kiss thy pallid cheek,
  And thou not know me nigh;
Asleep at last, and very meek,
  Who wert as proud as I.

III.

We did not dream, my Heart, and yet
   With what a pang we woke at last!
   We were not happy in the past
It is so bitter to forget.

We did not hope, my Soul, for Heaven;
   Yet now the hour of death is nigh;
   How hard, how strange it is to die
Like leaves along the tempest driven.

DEATH IN THE WORLD

The great white lilies in the grass
　Are pallid as the smile of death;
For they remember still—alas!
　The graves they sprang from underneath.

The Angels up in heaven are pale—
　For all have died, when all is said;
Nor shall the lutes of Eden avail
　To let them dream they are not dead.

ELYSIUM

Into the valley of Death am I come,
Into the asphodel meadow,
Where in the grass there is never a tomb,
Where there is rest and shadow!

All of the world is estranged to my eyes,
Scarce can I see you or hear you—
You that are far from my faint Paradise—
Though I am with you and near you.

All that I hoped for and all that I was,
Drops like a cloak from my shoulders,
Leaving the soul unencumbered to pass
Out of the ken of beholders.

Yea, in the valley of Death I awoke,
Pallid and strange as a vision,
All of my sorrow is vanished as smoke—
These are the valleys Elysian!

STORNELLI AND STRAMBOTTI

I.

Flower of the clove!
  Red rose the morning, and my heart was free;
Red sets the sun and, see, I die of Love!

* * *

O mandolines that thrill the moonlit street,
  O lemon flowers so faint and freshly blown,
O seas that lap a solemn music sweet
  Through all the pallid night against the stone,
O lovers tramping past with happy feet,
  O heart that hast a memory of thine own—
For Mercy's sake no more, no more repeat
  The word it is so hard to hear alone!

* * *

    Flower of the flax!
I cannot spin to-night; my heart is full.
Quick go the fingers where the lover lacks!

II.

Rosemary leaves!
She who remembers cannot love again;
She who remembers sits at home and grieves.

* * *

Love is a bird that breaks its voice with singing,
Love is a rose blown open till it fall,
Love is a bee that dies of its own stinging,
And Love the tinsel cross upon a pall.
Love is the Siren, towards a quicksand bringing
Enchanted fishermen that hear her call.
Love is a broken heart,—Farewell,—the wringing
Of dying hands. Ah, do not love at all!

* * *

Flower of a flower!
My heart alone may guess my lover's name,
Or where we met or when the happiest hour!

PRINCESSES

How did they feel, I wonder?
  Fairy princesses,—
Sending their lovers through
Danger as strange as new;
Caves full of flame and thunder,
  Fierce wildernesses?

I, of a simpler mind,
  Own them above me.
Dear, I could never ask
You for the lightest task—
So do I dread to find
  You may not love me!

LOVERS

So glad am I, my only Love,
   So glad that I could fly
Above the clouds and far enough—
   Join hands, and let us try!

We'll watch the world that spins below
   Amid a mist of stars;
Along the milky way we'll go
   Towards the heavenly bars.

And, smiling soft at one another,
   Sweet angels looking o'er
Shall cry, "These lovers love each other;
   Never were such before!"

A BALLAD OF FORGOTTEN TUNES

TO V. L.

Forgotten seers of lost repute
  That haunt the banks of Acheron,
Where have you dropped the broken lute
  You played in Troy or Calydon?
  O ye that sang in Babylon
By foreign willows cold and grey,
  Fall'n are the harps ye hanged thereon,
Dead are the tunes of yesterday!

De Coucy, is your music mute,
  The quaint old plain-chant woe-begone
That served so many a lover's suit?
  Oh, dead as Adam or Guédron!
  Then, sweet De Caurroy, try upon
Your virginals a virelay;
  Or play, Orlando, one pavonne—
Dead are the tunes of yesterday!

But ye whose praises none refute,
  Who have the immortal laurel won;—
Trill me your quavering close acute,
  Astorga, dear unhappy Don!
  One air, Galuppi! Sarti, one
So many fingers used to play!—
  Dead as the ladies of Villon,
Dead are the tunes of yesterday!

Envoy.

Vernon, in vain you stoop to con
The slender, faded notes to-day—
The Soul that dwelt in them is gone:
Dead are the tunes of yesterday!

CELIA'S HOME-COMING

Maidens, kilt your skirts and go
  Down the stormy garden-ways,
Pluck the last sweet pinks that blow,
  Gather roses, gather bays,
Since our Celia comes to-day
That has been too long away.

Crowd her chamber with your sweets—
  Not a flower but grows for her!
Make her bed with linen sheets
  That have lain in lavender;
Light a fire before she come
Lest she find us chill at home.

Ah, what joy when Celia stands
  By the leaping blaze at last,
Stooping down to warm her hands
  All benumbed with the blast,
While we hide her cloak away
To assure us she shall stay.

Cyder bring and cowslip wine,
  Fruits and flavours from the East,
Pears and pippins too, and fine
  Saffron loaves to make a feast:
China dishes, silver cups,
For the board where Celia sups!

Then, when all the feasting's done,
   She shall draw us round the blaze,
Laugh, and tell us every one
   Of her far triumphant days—
Celia, out of doors a star,
By the hearth a holier Lar!

ALTERNATIVES

Dearest, should I love you more
  If you understood me?
If, when I am sick and sore,
Straightway you divined wherefore,
Then with herbs and healing store
  Of your love imbued me?

Nay, I have instead, you know,
  In your heart an arbour,
Where the great winds never go
That about my spirit blow;
Where the sweet wild roses grow,
  Sweeter thrushes harbour.

What a joy at last to rest
  Safe therein from sorrow!
What a spur when sore distressed,
To at last attain your breast!
When the night is loneliest
  What a hope of morrow!

DRYADS

The Dryads dwell in Easter woods,
   Though mortals may not see them there;
They haunt those rustling solitudes,
   And love the solemn valleys where
   The bracken mocks their tawny hair.

And where the rushes make a hedge
   With flowering lilies round the lake,
They come to shelter in the sedge;
   They dip their shining feet and slake
   Their thirst where shallow waters break.

But through the sultry noon their home
   Surrounds some smooth old beechen stem.
Behold how thick the empty dome
   Is heaped with russet leaves for them,
   Where burr or thistle never came!

And there they lie in languid flocks,
   A drift of sweetness unespied;
They dream among their tawny locks
   Until the welcome eventide
   Breathe freshly through the woods outside.

And then a gleam of white is seen
   Among the huge old ilex-boughs;
The Dryads love its sombre green;
   They make the tree their summer-house,
   And there they swing and there carouse.

But, if the tender moon by chance
   Come up the skies with silver feet,
They spring upon the ground and dance
   Where most the turf is thick and sweet,—
   And would that we were there to see 't!

But, ah! if any woodman find
   A Dryad hid about a tree,
He drops his hatchet, stricken blind—
   I know not why, unless it be
   They are Immortals, and not he!

A ROSE

I.

She is a rose indeed!
  But I'll not take her—
I'll pluck me any weed:
  How could I break her?

Ay, she's the sweetest song!
  I'll sing it never.
Could I such music wrong
  With rude endeavour?

II.

Yet since you loved me, O my flower, my rose,
  Why could I not be dumb and let you love?
Why must I fling you all my passionate woes,
  The scorn, the anguish, the remorse thereof,
Down at your timid feet, too soft to tread
These brambles where I bow my desolate head.

The Picture of Dorian Gray

Oscar Wilde

CHAPTER I.

THE STUDIO WAS filled with the rich odour of roses, and when the light summer wind stirred amidst the trees of the garden there came through the open door the heavy scent of the lilac, or the more delicate perfume of the pink-flowering thorn.

From the corner of the divan of Persian saddlebags on which he was lying, smoking, as was his custom, innumerable cigarettes, Lord Henry Wotton could just catch the gleam of the honey-sweet and honey-coloured blossoms of a laburnum, whose tremulous branches seemed hardly able to bear the burden of a beauty so flame-like as theirs; and now and then the fantastic shadows of birds in flight flitted across the long tussore-silk curtains that were stretched in front of the huge window, producing a kind of momentary Japanese effect, and making him think of those pallid jade-faced painters of Tokio who, through the medium of an art that is necessarily immobile, seek to convey the sense of swiftness and motion. The sullen murmur of the bees shouldering their way through the long unmown grass, or circling with monotonous insistence round the dusty gilt horns of the straggling woodbine, seemed to make the stillness more oppressive. The dim roar of London was like the bourdon note of a distant organ.

In the centre of the room, clamped to an upright easel, stood the full-length portrait of a young man of extraordinary personal beauty, and in front of it, some little distance away, was sitting the artist himself, Basil Hallward, whose sudden disappearance some years ago caused, at the time, such public excitement, and gave rise to so many strange conjectures.

As the painter looked at the gracious and comely form he had so skilfully mirrored in his art, a smile of pleasure passed across his face, and seemed about to linger there. But he suddenly started up, and, closing his eyes, placed his fingers upon the lids, as though he sought to imprison within his brain some curious dream from which he feared he might awake.

"It is your best work, Basil, the best thing you have ever done," said Lord Henry, languidly. "You must certainly send it next year to the Grosvenor. The Academy is too large and too vulgar. Whenever I have gone there, there have been either so many people that I have not been able to see the pictures, which was dreadful, or so many pictures that I have not been able to see the people, which was worse. The Grosvenor is really the only place."

"I don't think I shall send it anywhere," he answered, tossing his head back in that odd way that used to make his friends laugh at him at Oxford. "No: I won't send it anywhere."

Lord Henry elevated his eyebrows, and looked at him in amazement through the thin blue wreaths of smoke that curled up in such fanciful whorls from his heavy opium-tainted cigarette. "Not send it anywhere? My dear fellow, why? Have you any reason? What odd chaps you painters are! You do anything in the world to gain a reputation. As soon as you have one, you seem to want to throw it away. It is silly of you, for there is only one thing in the world worse than being talked about, and that is not being talked about. A portrait like this would set you far above all the young men in England, and make the old men quite jealous, if old men are ever capable of any emotion."

"I know you will laugh at me," he replied, "but I really can't exhibit it. I have put too much of myself into it."

Lord Henry stretched himself out on the divan and laughed.

"Yes, I knew you would; but it is quite true, all the same."

"Too much of yourself in it! Upon my word, Basil, I didn't know you were so vain; and I really can't see any resemblance between you, with your rugged strong face and your coal-black hair, and this young Adonis, who looks as if he was made out of ivory and rose-leaves. Why, my dear Basil, he is a Narcissus, and you—well, of course you have an intellectual expression, and all that. But beauty, real beauty, ends where an intellectual expression begins. Intellect is in itself a mode of exaggeration, and destroys the harmony of any face. The moment one sits down to think, one becomes all nose, or all forehead, or something horrid. Look at the successful men in any of the learned professions. How perfectly hideous they are! Except, of course, in the Church. But then in the Church they don't think. A bishop keeps on saying at the age of eighty what he was told to say when he was a boy of eighteen, and as a natural consequence he always looks absolutely delightful. Your mysterious young friend, whose name you have never told me, but whose picture really fascinates me, never thinks. I feel quite sure of that. He is some brainless, beautiful creature, who should be always here in winter when we have no flowers to look at, and always here in summer when we want something to chill our intelligence. Don't flatter yourself, Basil: you are not in the least like him."

"You don't understand me, Harry," answered the artist. "Of course I am not like him. I know that perfectly well. Indeed, I should be sorry to look like him. You shrug your shoulders? I am telling you the truth. There is a fatality about all physical and intellectual distinction, the sort of fatality that seems to dog through history the faltering steps of kings. It is better not to be different from one's fellows. The ugly and the stupid have the best of it in this world. They can sit at their ease and gape at the play. If they know nothing of victory, they are at least spared the knowledge of defeat. They live as we all should live, undisturbed, indifferent, and without disquiet. They neither bring ruin upon others, nor ever receive it from alien hands. Your rank and wealth, Harry; my brains, such as they are—my art, whatever it may be worth; Dorian Gray's good looks—we shall all suffer for what the gods have given us, suffer terribly."

"Dorian Gray? Is that his name?" asked Lord Henry, walking across the studio towards Basil Hallward.

"Yes, that is his name. I didn't intend to tell it to you."

"But why not?"

"Oh, I can't explain. When I like people immensely I never tell their names to any one. It is like surrendering a part of them. I have grown to love secrecy. It seems to be the one thing that can make modern life mysterious or marvellous to us. The commonest thing is delightful if one only hides it. When I leave town now I never tell my people where I am going. If I did, I would lose all my pleasure. It is a silly habit, I dare say, but somehow it seems to bring a great deal of romance into one's life. I suppose you think me awfully foolish about it?"

"Not at all," answered Lord Henry, "not at all, my dear Basil. You seem to forget that I am married, and the one charm of marriage is that it makes a life of deception absolutely necessary for both parties. I never know where my wife is, and my wife never knows what I am doing. When we meet—we do meet occasionally, when we dine out together, or go down to the Duke's—we tell each other the most absurd stories with the most serious faces. My wife is very good at it—much better, in fact, than I am. She never gets confused over her dates, and I always do. But when she does find me out, she makes no row at all. I sometimes wish she would; but she merely laughs at me."

"I hate the way you talk about your married life, Harry," said Basil Hallward, strolling towards the door that led into the garden. "I believe that you are really a very good husband, but that you are thoroughly ashamed of your own virtues. You are an extraordinary fellow. You never say a moral thing, and you never do a wrong thing. Your cynicism is simply a pose."

"Being natural is simply a pose, and the most irritating pose I know," cried Lord Henry, laughing; and the two young men went out into the garden together, and ensconced themselves on a long bamboo seat that stood in the shade of a tall laurel bush. The sunlight slipped over the polished leaves. In the grass, white daisies were tremulous.

After a pause, Lord Henry pulled out his watch. "I am afraid I must be going, Basil," he murmured, "and before I go, I insist on your answering a question I put to you some time ago."

"What is that?" said the painter, keeping his eyes fixed on the ground.

"You know quite well."

"I do not, Harry."

"Well, I will tell you what it is. I want you to explain to me why you won't exhibit Dorian Gray's picture. I want the real reason."

"I told you the real reason."

"No, you did not. You said it was because there was too much of yourself in it. Now, that is childish."

"Harry," said Basil Hallward, looking him straight in the face, "every portrait that is painted with feeling is a portrait of the artist, not of the sitter. The sitter is merely the accident, the occasion. It is not he who is revealed by the painter; it is rather the painter who, on the coloured canvas, reveals himself. The reason I will not exhibit this picture is that I am afraid that I have shown in it the secret of my own soul."

Lord Henry laughed. "And what is that?" he asked.

"I will tell you," said Hallward; but an expression of perplexity came over his face.

"I am all expectation, Basil," continued his companion, glancing at him.

"Oh, there is really very little to tell, Harry," answered the painter; "and I am afraid you will hardly understand it. Perhaps you will hardly believe it."

Lord Henry smiled, and leaning down, plucked a pink-petalled daisy from the grass, and examined it. "I am quite sure I shall understand it," he replied, gazing intently at the little golden white-feathered disk, "and as for believing things, I can believe anything, provided that it is quite incredible."

The wind shook some blossoms from the trees, and the heavy lilac-blooms, with their clustering stars, moved to and fro in the languid air. A grasshopper began to chirrup by the wall, and like a blue thread a long thin dragon-fly floated past on its brown gauze wings. Lord Henry felt as if he could hear Basil Hallward's heart beating, and wondered what was coming.

"The story is simply this," said the painter after some time. "Two months ago I went to a crush at Lady Brandon's. You know we poor artists have to show ourselves in society from time to time, just to remind the public that we are not savages. With an evening coat and a white tie, as you told me once, anybody, even a stock-broker, can gain a reputation for being civilized. Well, after I had been in the room about ten minutes, talking to huge overdressed dowagers and tedious Academicians, I suddenly became conscious that some one was looking at me. I turned halfway round, and saw Dorian Gray for the first time. When our eyes met, I felt that I was growing pale. A curious sensation of terror came over me. I knew that I had come face to face with some one whose mere personality was so fascinating that, if I allowed it to do so, it would absorb my whole nature, my whole soul, my very art itself. I did not want any external influence in my life. You know yourself, Harry, how independent I am by nature. I have always been my own master; had at least always been so, till I met Dorian Gray. Then——but I don't know how to explain it to you. Something seemed to tell me that I was on the verge of a terrible crisis in my life. I had a strange feeling that Fate had in store for me exquisite joys and exquisite sorrows. I grew afraid, and turned to quit the room. It was not conscience that made me do so: it was a sort of cowardice. I take no credit to myself for trying to escape."

"Conscience and cowardice are really the same things, Basil. Conscience is the trade-name of the firm. That is all."

"I don't believe that, Harry, and I don't believe you do either. However, whatever was my motive—and it may have been pride, for I used to be very proud—I certainly struggled to the door. There, of course, I stumbled against Lady Brandon. 'You are not going to run away so soon, Mr. Hallward?' she screamed out. You know her curiously shrill voice?"

"Yes; she is a peacock in everything but beauty," said Lord Henry, pulling the daisy to bits with his long, nervous fingers.

"I could not get rid of her. She brought me up to Royalties, and people with Stars and Garters, and elderly ladies with gigantic tiaras and parrot noses. She spoke of me as her dearest friend. I had only met her once before, but she took it into her head to lionize me. I believe some picture of mine had made a great success at the time, at least had been chattered about in the penny newspapers, which is the nineteenth-century standard of immortality. Suddenly I found myself face to face with the young man whose personality had so strangely stirred me. We were quite close, almost touching. Our eyes met again. It was reckless of me, but I asked Lady Brandon to introduce me to him. Perhaps it was not so reckless, after all. It was simply inevitable. We would have spoken to each other without any introduction. I am sure of that. Dorian told me so afterwards. He, too, felt that we were destined to know each other."

"And how did Lady Brandon describe this wonderful young man?" asked his companion. "I know she goes in for giving a rapid *précis* of all her guests. I remember her bringing me up to a truculent and red-faced old gentleman covered all over with orders and ribbons, and hissing into my ear, in a tragic whisper which must have been perfectly audible to everybody in the room, the most astounding details. I simply fled. I like to find out people for myself. But Lady Brandon treats her guests exactly as an auctioneer treats his goods. She either explains them entirely away, or tells one everything about them except what one wants to know."

"Poor Lady Brandon! You are hard on her, Harry!" said Hallward, listlessly.

"My dear fellow, she tried to found a *salon*, and only succeeded in opening a restaurant. How could I admire her? But tell me, what did she say about Mr. Dorian Gray?"

"Oh, something like, 'Charming boy—poor dear mother and I absolutely inseparable. Quite forget what he does—afraid he—doesn't do anything—oh, yes, plays the piano—or is it the violin, dear Mr. Gray?' Neither of us could help laughing, and we became friends at once."

"Laughter is not at all a bad beginning for a friendship, and it is far the best ending for one," said the young lord, plucking another daisy.

Hallward shook his head, "You don't understand what friendship is, Harry," he murmured—"or what enmity is, for that matter. You like every one; that is to say, you are indifferent to every one."

"How horribly unjust of you!" cried Lord Henry, tilting his hat back, and looking up at the little clouds that, like ravelled skeins of glossy white silk, were drifting across the hollowed turquoise of the summer sky. "Yes; horribly unjust of you. I make a great difference between people. I choose my friends for their good looks, my acquaintances for their good characters, and my enemies for their good intellects. A man cannot be too careful in the choice of his enemies. I have not got one who is a fool. They are all men of some intellectual power, and consequently they all appreciate me. Is that very vain of me? I think it is rather vain."

"I should think it was, Harry. But according to your category I must be merely an acquaintance."

"My dear old Basil, you are much more than an acquaintance."

"And much less than a friend. A sort of brother, I suppose?"

"Oh, brothers! I don't care for brothers. My elder brother won't die, and my younger brothers seem never to do anything else."

"Harry!" exclaimed Hallward, frowning.

"My dear fellow, I am not quite serious. But I can't help detesting my relations. I suppose it comes from the fact that none of us can stand other people having the same faults as ourselves. I quite sympathize with the rage of the English democracy against what they call the vices of the upper orders. The masses feel that drunkenness, stupidity, and immorality should be their own special property, and that if any one of us makes an ass of himself he is poaching on their preserves. When poor Southwark got into the Divorce Court, their indignation was quite magnificent. And yet I don't suppose that ten cent. of the proletariat live correctly."

"I don't agree with a single word that you have said, and, what is more, Harry, I feel sure you don't either."

Lord Henry stroked his pointed brown beard, and tapped the toe of his patent-leather boot with a tasselled ebony cane. "How English you are Basil! That is the second time you have made that observation. If one puts forward an idea to a true Englishman—always a rash thing to do—he never dreams of considering whether the idea is right or wrong. The only thing he considers of any importance is whether one believes it oneself. Now, the value of an idea has nothing whatsoever to do with the sincerity of the man who expresses it. Indeed, the probabilities are that the more insincere the man is, the more purely intellectual will the idea be, as in that case it will not be coloured by either his wants, his desires, or his prejudices. However, I don't propose to discuss politics, sociology, or metaphysics with you. I like persons better than principles, and I like persons with no principles better than anything else in the world. Tell me more about Mr. Dorian Gray. How often do you see him?"

"Every day. I couldn't be happy if I didn't see him every day. He is absolutely necessary to me."

"How extraordinary! I thought you would never care for anything but your art."

"He is all my art to me now," said the painter, gravely. "I sometimes think, Harry, that there are only two eras of any importance in the world's history. The first is the appearance of a new medium for art, and the second is the appearance of a new personality for art also. What the invention of oil-painting was to the Venetians, the face of Antinoüs was to late Greek sculpture, and the face of Dorian Gray will some day be to me. It is not merely that I paint from him, draw from him, sketch from him. Of course I have done all that. But he is much more to me than a model or a sitter. I won't tell you that I am dissatisfied with what I have done of him, or that his beauty is such that Art cannot express it. There is nothing that Art cannot express, and I know that the work I have done, since I met Dorian Gray, is good work, is the best work of my life. But in some curious way—I wonder will you understand me?—his personality has suggested to me an entirely new manner in art, an entirely new mode of style. I see things differently, I think of them differently. I can now recreate life in a way that was hidden from me before. 'A dream of form in days of thought':—who is it who says that? I forget; but it is what Dorian Gray has been to me. The merely visible presence of this lad—for he seems to me little more than a lad, though he is really over twenty—his merely visible presence—ah! I wonder can you realize all that that means? Unconsciously he defines for me the lines of a fresh school, a school that is to have in it all the passion of the romantic spirit, all the perfection of the spirit that is Greek. The harmony of soul and body—how much that is! We in our madness have separated the two, and have invented a realism that is vulgar, an ideality that is void. Harry! if you only knew what Dorian Gray is to me! You remember that landscape of mine, for which Agnew offered me such a huge price, but which I would not part with? It is one of the best things I have ever done. And why is it so? Because, while I was painting it, Dorian Gray sat beside me. Some subtle influence passed from him to me, and for the first time in my life I saw in the plain woodland the wonder I had always looked for, and always missed."

"Basil, this is extraordinary! I must see Dorian Gray."

Hallward got up from the seat, and walked up and down the garden. After some time he came back. "Harry," he said, "Dorian Gray is to me simply a motive in art. You might see nothing in him. I see everything in him. He is never more present in my work than when no image of him is there. He is a suggestion, as I have said, of a new manner. I find him in the curves of certain lines, in the loveliness and subtleties of certain colours. That is all."

"Then why won't you exhibit his portrait?" asked Lord Henry.

"Because, without intending it, I have put into it some expression of all this curious artistic idolatry, of which, of course, I have never cared to speak to him. He knows nothing about it. He shall never know anything about it. But the world might guess it; and I will not bare my soul to their shallow, prying eyes. My heart shall never be put under their microscope. There is too much of myself in the thing, Harry—too much of myself!"

"Poets are not so scrupulous as you are. They know how useful passion is for publication. Nowadays a broken heart will run to many editions."

"I hate them for it," cried Hallward. "An artist should create beautiful things, but should put nothing of his own life into them. We live in an age when men treat art as if it were meant to be a form of autobiography. We have lost the abstract sense of beauty. Some day I will show the world what it is; and for that reason the world shall never see my portrait of Dorian Gray."

"I think you are wrong, Basil, but I won't argue with you. It is only the intellectually lost who ever argue. Tell me, is Dorian Gray very fond of you?"

The painter considered for a few moments. "He likes me," he answered after a pause; "I know he likes me. Of course I flatter him dreadfully. I find a strange pleasure in saying things to him that I know I shall be sorry for having said. As a rule, he is charming to me, and we sit in the studio and talk of a thousand things. Now and then, however, he is horribly thoughtless, and seems to take a real delight in giving me pain. Then I feel, Harry, that I have given away my whole soul to some one who treats it as if it were a flower to put in his coat, a bit of decoration to charm his vanity, an ornament for a summer's day."

"Days in summer, Basil, are apt to linger," murmured Lord Henry. "Perhaps you will tire sooner than he will. It is a sad thing to think of, but there is no doubt that Genius lasts longer than Beauty. That accounts for the fact that we all take such pains to over-educate ourselves. In the wild struggle for existence, we want to have something that endures, and so we fill our minds with rubbish and facts, in the silly hope of keeping our place. The thoroughly well-informed man—that is the modern ideal. And the mind of the thoroughly well-informed man is a dreadful thing. It is like a bric-à-brac shop, all monsters and dust, with everything priced above its proper value. I think you will tire first, all the same. Some day you will look at your friend, and he will seem to you to be a little out of drawing, or you won't like his tone of colour, or something. You will bitterly reproach him in your own heart, and seriously think that he has behaved very badly to you. The next time he calls, you will be perfectly cold and indifferent. It will be a great pity, for it will alter you. What you have told me is quite a romance, a romance of art one might call it, and the worst of having a romance of any kind is that it leaves one so unromantic."

"Harry, don't talk like that. As long as I live, the personality of Dorian Gray will dominate me. You can't feel what I feel. You change too often."

"Ah, my dear Basil, that is exactly why I can feel it. Those who are faithful know only the trivial side of love: it is the faithless who know love's tragedies." And Lord Henry struck a light on a dainty silver case, and began to smoke a cigarette with a self-conscious and satisfied air, as if he had summed up the world in a phrase. There was a rustle of chirruping sparrows in the green lacquer leaves of the ivy, and the blue cloud-shadows chased themselves across the grass like swallows. How pleasant it was in the garden! And how delightful other people's emotions were!—

much more delightful than their ideas, it seemed to him. One's own soul, and the passions of one's friends—those were the fascinating things in life. He pictured to himself with silent amusement the tedious luncheon that he had missed by staying so long with Basil Hallward. Had he gone to his aunt's, he would have been sure to have met Lord Goodbody there, and the whole conversation would have been about the feeding of the poor, and the necessity for model lodging-houses. Each class would have preached the importance of those virtues, for whose exercise there was no necessity in their own lives. The rich would have spoken on the value of thrift, and the idle grown eloquent over the dignity of labour. It was charming to have escaped all that! As he thought of his aunt, an idea seemed to strike him. He turned to Hallward, and said, "My dear fellow, I have just remembered."

"Remembered what, Harry?"

"Where I heard the name of Dorian Gray."

"Where was it?" asked Hallward, with a slight frown.

"Don't look so angry, Basil. It was at my aunt, Lady Agatha's. She told me she had discovered a wonderful young man, who was going to help her in the East End, and that his name was Dorian Gray. I am bound to state that she never told me he was good-looking. Women have no appreciation of good looks; at least, good women have not. She said that he was very earnest, and had a beautiful nature. I at once pictured to myself a creature with spectacles and lank hair, horribly freckled, and tramping about on huge feet. I wish I had known it was your friend."

"I am very glad you didn't, Harry."

"Why?"

"I don't want you to meet him."

"You don't want me to meet him?"

"No."

"Mr. Dorian Gray is in the studio, sir," said the butler, coming into the garden.

"You must introduce me now," cried Lord Henry, laughing.

The painter turned to his servant, who stood blinking in the sunlight. "Ask Mr. Gray to wait, Parker: I shall be in in a few moments." The man bowed, and went up the walk.

Then he looked at Lord Henry. "Dorian Gray is my dearest friend," he said. "He has a simple and beautiful nature. Your aunt was quite right in what she said of him. Don't spoil him. Don't try to influence him. Your influence would be bad. The world is wide, and has many marvellous people in it. Don't take away from me the one person who gives to my art whatever charm it possesses: my life as an artist depends on him. Mind, Harry, I trust you." He spoke very slowly, and the words seemed wrung out of him almost against his will.

"What nonsense you talk!" said Lord Henry, smiling, and, taking Hallward by the arm, he almost led him into the house.

CHAPTER II.

As THEY ENTERED they saw Dorian Gray. He was seated at the piano, with his back to them, turning over the pages of a volume of Schumann's "Forest Scenes." "You must lend me these, Basil," he cried. "I want to learn them. They are perfectly charming."

"That entirely depends on how you sit to-day, Dorian."

"Oh, I am tired of sitting, and I don't want a life-sized portrait of myself," answered the lad, swinging round on the music-stool, in a wilful, petulant manner. When he caught sight of Lord Henry, a faint blush coloured his cheeks for a moment, and he started up. "I beg your pardon, Basil, but I didn't know you had any one with you."

"This is Lord Henry Wotton, Dorian, an old Oxford friend of mine. I have just been telling him what a capital sitter you were, and now you have spoiled everything."

"You have not spoiled my pleasure in meeting you, Mr. Gray," said Lord Henry, stepping forward and extending his hand. "My aunt has often spoken to me about you. You are one of her favourites, and, I am afraid, one of her victims also."

"I am in Lady Agatha's black books at present," answered Dorian, with a funny look of penitence. "I promised to go to a club in Whitechapel with her last Tuesday, and I really forgot all about it. We were to have played a duet together—three duets, I believe. I don't know what she will say to me. I am far too frightened to call."

"Oh, I will make your peace with my aunt. She is quite devoted to you. And I don't think it really matters about your not being there. The audience probably thought it was a duet. When Aunt Agatha sits down to the piano she makes quite enough noise for two people."

"That is very horrid to her, and not very nice to me," answered Dorian, laughing.

Lord Henry looked at him. Yes, he was certainly wonderfully handsome, with his finely-curved scarlet lips, his frank blue eyes, his crisp gold hair. There was something in his face that made one trust him at once. All the candour of youth was there, as well as all youth's passionate purity. One felt that he had kept himself unspotted from the world. No wonder Basil Hallward worshipped him.

"You are too charming to go in for philanthropy, Mr. Gray—far too charming." And Lord Henry flung himself down on the divan, and opened his cigarette-case.

The painter had been busy mixing his colours and getting his brushes ready. He was looking worried, and when he heard Lord Henry's last remark he glanced at him, hesitated for a moment, and then said, "Harry, I want to finish this picture to-day. Would you think it awfully rude of me if I asked you to go away?"

Lord Henry smiled, and looked at Dorian Gray. "Am I to go, Mr. Gray?" he asked.

"Oh, please don't, Lord Henry. I see that Basil is in one of his sulky moods; and I can't bear him when he sulks. Besides, I want you to tell me why I should not go in for philanthropy."

"I don't know that I shall tell you that, Mr. Gray. It is so tedious a subject that one would have to talk seriously about it. But I certainly shall not run away, now that you have asked me to stop. You don't really mind, Basil, do you? You have often told me that you liked your sitters to have some one to chat to."

Hallward bit his lip. "If Dorian wishes it, of course you must stay. Dorian's whims are laws to everybody, except himself."

Lord Henry took up his hat and gloves. "You are very pressing, Basil, but I am afraid I must go. I have promised to meet a man at the Orleans. Good-bye, Mr. Gray. Come and see me some afternoon in Curzon Street. I am nearly always at home at five o'clock. Write to me when you are coming. I should be sorry to miss you."

"Basil," cried Dorian Gray, "if Lord Henry Wotton goes I shall go too. You never open your lips while you are painting, and it is horribly dull standing on a platform and trying to look pleasant. Ask him to stay. I insist upon it."

"Stay, Harry, to oblige Dorian, and to oblige me," said Hallward, gazing intently at his picture. "It is quite true, I never talk when I am working, and never listen either, and it must be dreadfully tedious for my unfortunate sitters. I beg you to stay."

"But what about my man at the Orleans?"

The painter laughed. "I don't think there will be any difficulty about that. Sit down again, Harry. And now, Dorian, get up on the platform, and don't move about too much, or pay any attention to what Lord Henry says. He has a very bad influence over all his friends, with the single exception of myself."

Dorian Gray stepped up on the dais, with the air of a young Greek martyr, and made a little *moue*[1] of discontent to Lord Henry, to whom he had rather taken a fancy. He was so unlike Basil. They made a delightful contrast. And he had such a beautiful voice. After a few moments he said to him, "Have you really a very bad influence, Lord Henry? As bad as Basil says?"

"There is no such thing as a good influence, Mr. Gray. All influence is immoral—immoral from the scientific point of view."

"Why?"

"Because to influence a person is to give him one's own soul. He does not think his natural thoughts, or burn with his natural passions. His virtues are not real to him. His sins, if there are such things as sins, are borrowed. He becomes an echo of some one else's music, an actor of a part that has not been written for him. The aim of life is self-development. To realize one's nature perfectly—that is what each of us is here for. People are afraid of themselves, nowadays. They have forgotten the highest of all duties, the duty that one owes to one's self. Of course they are charitable. They feed the hungry, and clothe the beggar. But their own souls starve, and are naked. Courage has gone out of our race. Perhaps we never really had it. The terror of society, which is the basis of morals, the terror of God, which is the secret of religion—these are the two things that govern us. And yet——"

"Just turn your head a little more to the right, Dorian, like a good boy," said the painter, deep in his work, and conscious only that a look had come into the lad's face that he had never seen there before.

"And yet," continued Lord Henry, in his low, musical voice, and with that graceful wave of the hand that was always so characteristic of him, and that he had even in his Eton days, "I believe that if one man were to live out his life fully and completely, were to give form to every feeling, expression to every thought, reality to every dream—I believe that the world would gain such a fresh impulse of joy that we would forget all the maladies of mediævalism, and return

[1] Pouting expression.

to the Hellenic ideal—to something finer, richer, than the Hellenic ideal, it may be. But the bravest man amongst us is afraid of himself. The mutilation of the savage has its tragic survival in the self-denial that mars our lives. We are punished for our refusals. Every impulse that we strive to strangle broods in the mind, and poisons us. The body sins once, and has done with its sin, for action is a mode of purification. Nothing remains then but the recollection of a pleasure, or the luxury of a regret. The only way to get rid of a temptation is to yield to it. Resist it, and your soul grows sick with longing for the things it has forbidden to itself, with desire for what its monstrous laws have made monstrous and unlawful. It has been said that the great events of the world take place in the brain. It is in the brain, and the brain only, that the great sins of the world take place also. You, Mr. Gray, you yourself, with your rose-red youth and your rose-white boyhood, you have had passions that have made you afraid, thoughts that have filled you with terror, day-dreams and sleeping dreams whose mere memory might stain your cheek with shame——"

"Stop!" faltered Dorian Gray, "stop! you bewilder me. I don't know what to say. There is some answer to you, but I cannot find it. Don't speak. Let me think. Or, rather, let me try not to think."

For nearly ten minutes he stood there, motionless, with parted lips, and eyes strangely bright. He was dimly conscious that entirely fresh influences were at work within him. Yet they seemed to him to have come really from himself. The few words that Basil's friend had said to him—words spoken by chance, no doubt, and with wilful paradox in them—had touched some secret chord that had never been touched before, but that he felt was now vibrating and throbbing to curious pulses.

Music had stirred him like that. Music had troubled him many times. But music was not articulate. It was not a new world, but rather another chaos, that it created in us. Words! Mere words! How terrible they were! How clear, and vivid, and cruel! One could not escape from them. And yet what a subtle magic there was in them! They seemed to be able to give a plastic form to formless things, and to have a music of their own as sweet as that of viol or of lute. Mere words! Was there anything so real as words?

Yes; there had been things in his boyhood that he had not understood. He understood them now. Life suddenly became fiery-coloured to him. It seemed to him that he had been walking in fire. Why had he not known it?

With his subtle smile, Lord Henry watched him. He knew the precise psychological moment when to say nothing. He felt intensely interested. He was amazed at the sudden impression that his words had produced, and, remembering a book that he had read when he was sixteen, a book which had revealed to him much that he had not known before, he wondered whether Dorian Gray was passing through a similar experience. He had merely shot an arrow into the air. Had it hit the mark? How fascinating the lad was!

Hallward painted away with that marvellous bold touch of his, that had the true refinement and perfect delicacy that in art, at any rate, comes only from strength. He was unconscious of the silence.

"Basil, I am tired of standing," cried Dorian Gray, suddenly. "I must go out and sit in the garden. The air is stifling here."

"My dear fellow, I am so sorry. When I am painting, I can't think of anything else. But you never sat better. You were perfectly still. And I have caught the effect I wanted—the half-parted lips, and the bright look in the eyes. I don't know what Harry has been saying to you, but he has certainly made you have the most wonderful expression. I suppose he has been paying you compliments. You mustn't believe a word that he says."

"He has certainly not been paying me compliments. Perhaps that is the reason that I don't believe anything he has told me."

"You know you believe it all," said Lord Henry, looking at him with his dreamy, languorous eyes. "I will go out to the garden with you. It is horribly hot in the studio. Basil, let us have something iced to drink, something with strawberries in it."

"Certainly, Harry. Just touch the bell, and when Parker comes I will tell him what you want. I have got to work up this background, so I will join you later on. Don't keep Dorian too long. I have never been in better form for painting than I am to-day. This is going to be my masterpiece. It is my masterpiece as it stands."

Lord Henry went out to the garden, and found Dorian Gray burying his face in the great cool lilac-blossoms, feverishly drinking in their perfume as if it had been wine. He came close to him, and put his hand upon his shoulder. "You are quite right to do that," he murmured. "Nothing can cure the soul but the senses, just as nothing can cure the senses but the soul."

The lad started and drew back. He was bare-headed, and the leaves had tossed his rebellious curls and tangled all their gilded threads. There was a look of fear in his eyes, such as people have when they are suddenly awakened. His finely-chiselled nostrils quivered, and some hidden nerve shook the scarlet of his lips and left them trembling.

"Yes," continued Lord Henry, "that is one of the great secrets of life—to cure the soul by means of the senses, and the senses by means of the soul. You are a wonderful creation. You know more than you think you know, just as you know less than you want to know."

Dorian Gray frowned and turned his head away. He could not help liking the tall, graceful young man who was standing by him. His romantic olive-coloured face and worn expression interested him. There was something in his low, languid voice that was absolutely fascinating. His cool, white, flower-like hands, even, had a curious charm. They moved, as he spoke, like music, and seemed to have a language of their own. But he felt afraid of him, and ashamed of being afraid. Why had it been left for a stranger to reveal him to himself? He had known Basil Hallward for months, but the friendship between them had never altered him. Suddenly there had come some one across his life who seemed to have disclosed to him life's mystery. And, yet, what was there to be afraid of? He was not a schoolboy or a girl. It was absurd to be frightened.

"Let us go and sit in the shade," said Lord Henry. "Parker has brought out the drinks, and if you stay any longer in this glare you will be quite spoiled, and Basil will never paint you again. You really must not allow yourself to become sunburnt. It would be unbecoming."

"What can it matter?" cried Dorian Gray, laughing, as he sat down on the seat at the end of the garden.

"It should matter everything to you, Mr. Gray."

"Why?"

"Because you have the most marvellous youth, and youth is the one thing worth having."

"I don't feel that, Lord Henry."

"No, you don't feel it now. Some day, when you are old and wrinkled and ugly, when thought has seared your forehead with its lines, and passion branded your lips with its hideous fires, you will feel it, you will feel it terribly. Now, wherever you go, you charm the world. Will it always be so? . . . You have a wonderfully beautiful face, Mr. Gray. Don't frown. You have. And Beauty is a form of Genius—is higher, indeed, than Genius, as it needs no explanation. It is of the great facts of the world, like sunlight, or spring-time, or the reflection in dark waters of that silver shell we call the moon. It cannot be questioned. It has its divine right of sovereignty. It makes princes of those who have it. You smile? Ah! when you have lost it you won't smile. . . . People say sometimes that Beauty is only superficial. That may be so. But at least it is not so superficial as Thought is. To me, Beauty is the wonder of wonders. It is only shallow people who do not judge by appearances. The true mystery of the world is the visible, not the invisible. . . . Yes, Mr. Gray, the gods have been good to you. But what the gods give they quickly take away. You have only a few years in which to live really, perfectly, and fully. When your youth goes, your beauty will go with it, and then you will suddenly discover that there are no triumphs left for you, or have to content yourself with those mean triumphs that the memory of your past will make more bitter than defeats. Every month as it wanes brings you nearer to something dreadful. Time is jealous of you, and wars against your lilies and your roses. You will become sallow, and hollow-cheeked, and dull-eyed. You will suffer horribly. . . . Ah! realize your youth while you have it. Don't squander the gold of your days, listening to the tedious, trying to improve the hopeless failure, or giving away your life to the ignorant, the common, and the vulgar. These are the sickly aims, the false ideals, of our age. Live! Live the wonderful life that is in you! Let nothing be lost upon you. Be always searching for new sensations. Be afraid of nothing. . . . A new Hedonism—that is what our century wants. You might be its visible symbol. With your personality there is nothing you could not do. The world belongs to you for a season. . . . The moment I met you I saw that you were quite unconscious of what you really are, of what you really might be. There was so much in you that charmed me that I felt I must tell you something about yourself. I thought how tragic it would be if you were wasted. For there is such a little time that your youth will last—such a little time. The common hill-flowers wither, but they blossom again. The laburnum will be as yellow next June as it is now. In a month there will be purple stars on the clematis, and year after year the green night of its leaves will hold its purple stars. But we never get back our youth. The pulse of joy that beats in us at twenty, becomes sluggish. Our limbs fail, our senses rot. We degenerate into hideous puppets, haunted by the memory of the passions of which we were too much afraid, and the exquisite temptations that we had not the courage to yield to. Youth! Youth! There is absolutely nothing in the world but youth!"

Dorian Gray listened, open-eyed and wondering. The spray of lilac fell from his hand upon the gravel. A furry bee came and buzzed round it for a moment. Then it began to scramble all over the oval stellated globe of the tiny blossoms. He watched it with that strange interest in trivial things that we try to develop when things of high import make us afraid, or when we are stirred by some new emotion for which we cannot find expression, or when some thought that terrifies us lays sudden siege to the brain and calls on us to yield. After a time the bee flew away. He saw it creeping into the stained trumpet of a Tyrian convolvulus. The flower seemed to quiver, and then swayed gently to and fro.

Suddenly the painter appeared at the door of the studio, and made staccato signs for them to come in. They turned to each other, and smiled.

"I am waiting," he cried. "Do come in. The light is quite perfect, and you can bring your drinks."

They rose up, and sauntered down the walk together. Two green-and-white butterflies fluttered past them, and in the pear-tree at the corner of the garden a thrush began to sing.

"You are glad you have met me, Mr. Gray," said Lord Henry, looking at him.

"Yes, I am glad now. I wonder shall I always be glad?"

"Always! That is a dreadful word. It makes me shudder when I hear it. Women are so fond of using it. They spoil every romance by trying to make it last for ever. It is a meaningless word, too. The only difference between a caprice and a life-long passion is that the caprice lasts a little longer."

As they entered the studio, Dorian Gray put his hand upon Lord Henry's arm. "In that case, let our friendship be a caprice," he murmured, flushing at his own boldness, then stepped up on the platform and resumed his pose.

Lord Henry flung himself into a large wicker arm-chair, and watched him. The sweep and dash of the brush on the canvas made the only sound that broke the stillness, except when, now and then, Hallward stepped back to look at his work from a distance. In the slanting beams that streamed through the open doorway the dust danced and was golden. The heavy scent of the roses seemed to brood over everything.

After about a quarter of an hour Hallward stopped painting, looked for a long time at Dorian Gray, and then for a long time at the picture, biting the end of one of his huge brushes, and frowning. "It is quite finished," he cried at last, and stooping down he wrote his name in long vermilion letters on the left-hand corner of the canvas.

Lord Henry came over and examined the picture. It was certainly a wonderful work of art, and a wonderful likeness as well.

"My dear fellow, I congratulate you most warmly," he said. "It is the finest portrait of modern times. Mr. Gray, come over and look at yourself."

The lad started, as if awakened from some dream. "Is it really finished?" he murmured, stepping down from the platform.

"Quite finished," said the painter. "And you have sat splendidly to-day. I am awfully obliged to you."

"That is entirely due to me," broke in Lord Henry. "Isn't it, Mr. Gray?"

Dorian made no answer, but passed listlessly in front of his picture and turned towards it. When he saw it he drew back, and his cheeks flushed for a moment with pleasure. A look of joy came into his eyes, as if he had recognized himself for the first time. He stood there motionless and in wonder, dimly conscious that Hallward was speaking to him, but not catching the meaning of his words. The sense of his own beauty came on him like a revelation. He had never felt it before. Basil Hallward's compliments had seemed to him to be merely the charming exaggerations of friendship. He had listened to them, laughed at them, forgotten them. They had not influenced his nature. Then had come Lord Henry Wotton with his strange panegyric on youth, his terrible warning of its brevity. That had stirred him at the time, and now, as he stood gazing at the shadow of his own loveliness, the full reality of the description flashed across him. Yes, there would be a day when his face would be wrinkled and wizen, his eyes dim and colourless, the grace of his figure broken and deformed. The scarlet would pass away from his lips, and the gold steal from his hair. The life that was to make his soul would mar his body. He would become dreadful, hideous, and uncouth.

As he thought of it, a sharp pang of pain struck through him like a knife, and made each delicate fibre of his nature quiver. His eyes deepened into amethyst, and across them came a mist of tears. He felt as if a hand of ice had been laid upon his heart.

"Don't you like it?" cried Hallward at last, stung a little by the lad's silence, not understanding what it meant.

"Of course he likes it," said Lord Henry. "Who wouldn't like it? It is one of the greatest things in modern art. I will give you anything you like to ask for it. I must have it."

"It is not my property, Harry."

"Whose property is it?"

"Dorian's, of course," answered the painter.

"He is a very lucky fellow."

"How sad it is!" murmured Dorian Gray, with his eyes still fixed upon his own portrait. "How sad it is! I shall grow old, and horrible, and dreadful. But this picture will remain always young. It will never be older than this particular day of June. . . . If it were only the other way! If it were I who was to be always young, and the picture that was to grow old! For that—for that—I would give everything! Yes, there is nothing in the whole world I would not give! I would give my soul for that!"

"You would hardly care for such an arrangement, Basil," cried Lord Henry, laughing. "It would be rather hard lines on your work."

"I should object very strongly, Harry," said Hallward.

Dorian Gray turned and looked at him. "I believe you would, Basil. You like your art better than your friends. I am no more to you than a green bronze figure. Hardly as much, I dare say."

The painter stared in amazement. It was so unlike Dorian to speak like that. What had happened? He seemed quite angry. His face was flushed and his cheeks burning.

"Yes," he continued, "I am less to you than your ivory Hermes or your silver Faun. You will like them always. How long will you like me? Till I have my first wrinkle, I suppose. I know, now, that when one loses one's good looks, whatever they may be, one loses everything. Your picture has taught me that. Lord Henry Wotton is perfectly right. Youth is the only thing worth having. When I find that I am growing old, I shall kill myself."

Hallward turned pale, and caught his hand. "Dorian! Dorian!" he cried, "don't talk like that. I have never had such a friend as you, and I shall never have such another. You are not jealous of material things, are you?—you who are finer than any of them!"

"I am jealous of everything whose beauty does not die. I am jealous of the portrait you have painted of me. Why should it keep what I must lose? Every moment that passes takes something from me, and gives something to it. Oh, if it were only the other way! If the picture could change, and I could be always what I am now! Why did you paint it? It will mock me some day—mock me horribly!" The hot tears welled into his eyes; he tore his hand away, and, flinging himself on the divan, he buried his face in the cushions, as though he was praying.

"This is your doing, Harry," said the painter, bitterly.

Lord Henry shrugged his shoulders. "It is the real Dorian Gray—that is all."

"It is not."

"If it is not, what have I to do with it?"

"You should have gone away when I asked you," he muttered.

"I stayed when you asked me," was Lord Henry's answer.

"Harry, I can't quarrel with my two best friends at once, but between you both you have made me hate the finest piece of work I have ever done, and I will destroy it. What is it but canvas and colour? I will not let it come across our three lives and mar them."

Dorian Gray lifted his golden head from the pillow, and with pallid face and tear-stained eyes looked at him, as he walked over to the deal painting-table that was set beneath the high curtained window. What was he doing there? His fingers were straying about among the litter of tin tubes and dry brushes, seeking for something. Yes, it was for the long palette-knife, with its thin blade of lithe steel. He had found it at last. He was going to rip up the canvas.

With a stifled sob the lad leaped from the couch, and, rushing over to Hallward, tore the knife out of his hand, and flung it to the end of the studio. "Don't, Basil, don't!" he cried. "It would be murder!"

"I am glad you appreciate my work at last, Dorian," said the painter, coldly, when he had recovered from his surprise. "I never thought you would."

"Appreciate it? I am in love with it, Basil. It is part of myself. I feel that."

"Well, as soon as you are dry, you shall be varnished, and framed, and sent home. Then you can do what you like with yourself." And he walked across the room and rang the bell for tea. "You will have tea, of course, Dorian? And so will you, Harry? Or do you object to such simple pleasures?"

"I adore simple pleasures," said Lord Henry. "They are the last refuge of the complex. But I don't like scenes, except on the stage. What absurd fellows you are, both of you! I wonder who it was defined man as a rational animal. It was the most premature definition ever given. Man is many things, but he is not rational. I am glad he is not, after all: though I wish you chaps would not squabble over the picture. You had much better let me have it, Basil. This silly boy doesn't really want it, and I really do."

"If you let any one have it but me, Basil, I shall never forgive you!" cried Dorian Gray; "and I don't allow people to call me a silly boy."

"You know the picture is yours, Dorian. I gave it to you before it existed."

"And you know you have been a little silly, Mr. Gray, and that you don't really object to being reminded that you are extremely young."

"I should have objected very strongly this morning, Lord Henry."

"Ah! this morning! You have lived since then."

There came a knock at the door, and the butler entered with a laden tea-tray and set it down upon a small Japanese table. There was a rattle of cups and saucers and the hissing of a fluted Georgian urn. Two globe-shaped china dishes were brought in by a page. Dorian Gray went over and poured out the tea. The two men sauntered languidly to the table, and examined what was under the covers.

"Let us go to the theatre to-night," said Lord Henry. "There is sure to be something on, somewhere. I have promised to dine at White's, but it is only with an old friend, so I can send him a wire to say that I am ill, or that I am prevented from coming in consequence of a subsequent engagement. I think that would be a rather nice excuse: it would have all the surprise of candour."

"It is such a bore putting on one's dress-clothes," muttered Hallward. "And, when one has them on, they are so horrid."

"Yes," answered Lord Henry, dreamily, "the costume of the nineteenth century is detestable. It is so sombre, so depressing. Sin is the only real colour-element left in modern life."

"You really must not say things like that before Dorian, Harry."

"Before which Dorian? The one who is pouring out tea for us, or the one in the picture?"

"Before either."

"I should like to come to the theatre with you, Lord Henry," said the lad.

"Then you shall come; and you will come too, Basil, won't you?"

"I can't, really. I would sooner not. I have a lot of work to do."

"Well, then, you and I will go alone, Mr. Gray."

"I should like that awfully."

The painter bit his lip and walked over, cup in hand, to the picture. "I shall stay with the real Dorian," he said, sadly.

"Is it the real Dorian?" cried the original of the portrait, strolling across to him. "Am I really like that?"

"Yes; you are just like that."

"How wonderful, Basil!"

"At least you are like it in appearance. But it will never alter," sighed Hallward. "That is something."

"What a fuss people make about fidelity!" exclaimed Lord Henry. "Why, even in love it is purely a question for physiology. It has nothing to do with our own will. Young men want to be faithful, and are not; old men want to be faithless, and cannot: that is all one can say."

"Don't go to the theatre to-night, Dorian," said Hallward. "Stop and dine with me."

"I can't, Basil."

"Why?"

"Because I have promised Lord Henry Wotton to go with him."

"He won't like you the better for keeping your promises. He always breaks his own. I beg you not to go."

Dorian Gray laughed and shook his head.

"I entreat you."

The lad hesitated, and looked over at Lord Henry, who was watching them from the tea-table with an amused smile.

"I must go, Basil," he answered.

"Very well," said Hallward; and he went over and laid down his cup on the tray. "It is rather late, and, as you have to dress, you had better lose no time. Good-bye, Harry. Good-bye, Dorian. Come and see me soon. Come to-morrow."

"Certainly."

"You won't forget?"

"No, of course not," cried Dorian.

"And . . . Harry!"

"Yes, Basil?"

"Remember what I asked you, when we were in the garden this morning."

"I have forgotten it."

"I trust you."

"I wish I could trust myself," said Lord Henry, laughing. "Come, Mr. Gray, my hansom is outside, and I can drop you at your own place. Good-bye, Basil. It has been a most interesting afternoon."

As the door closed behind them, the painter flung himself down on a sofa, and a look of pain came into his face. . . .

CHAPTER IX.

As he was sitting at breakfast next morning, Basil Hallward was shown into the room.

"I am so glad I have found you, Dorian," he said, gravely. "I called last night, and they told me you were at the Opera. Of course I knew that was impossible. But I wish you had left word where you had really gone to. I passed a dreadful evening, half afraid that one tragedy might be followed by another. I think you might have telegraphed for me when you heard of it first. I read of it quite by chance in a late edition of *The Globe*, that I picked up at the club. I came here at once, and was miserable at not finding you. I can't tell you how heart-broken I am about the whole thing. I know what you must suffer. But where were you? Did you go down and see the girl's mother? For a moment I thought of following you there. They gave the address in the paper. Somewhere in the Euston Road, isn't it? But I was afraid of intruding upon a sorrow that I could not lighten. Poor woman! What a state she must be in! And her only child, too! What did she say about it all?"

"My dear Basil, how do I know?" murmured Dorian Gray, sipping some pale-yellow wine from a delicate gold-beaded bubble of Venetian glass, and looking dreadfully bored. "I was at the Opera. You should have come on there. I met Lady Gwendolen, Harry's sister, for the first time. We were in her box. She is perfectly charming; and Patti sang divinely. Don't talk about horrid subjects. If one doesn't talk about a thing, it has never happened. It is simply expression, as Harry says, that gives reality to things. I may mention that she was not the woman's only child. There is a son, a charming fellow, I believe. But he is not on the stage. He is a sailor, or something. And now, tell me about yourself and what you are painting."

"You went to the Opera?" said Hallward, speaking very slowly, and with a strained touch of pain in his voice. "You went to the Opera while Sibyl Vane was lying dead in some sordid lodging? You can talk to me of other women being charming, and of Patti singing divinely, before the girl you loved has even the quiet of a grave to sleep in? Why, man, there are horrors in store for that little white body of hers!"

"Stop, Basil! I won't hear it!" cried Dorian, leaping to his feet. "You must not tell me about things. What is done is done. What is past is past."

"You call yesterday the past?"

"What has the actual lapse of time got to do with it? It is only shallow people who require years to get rid of an emotion. A man who is master of himself can end a sorrow as easily as he can invent a pleasure. I don't want to be at the mercy of my emotions. I want to use them, to enjoy them, and to dominate them."

"Dorian, this is horrible! Something has changed you completely. You look exactly the same wonderful boy who, day after day, used to come down to my studio to sit for his picture. But you were simple, natural, and affectionate then. You were the most unspoiled creature in the whole world. Now, I don't know what has come over you. You talk as if you had no heart, no pity in you. It is all Harry's influence. I see that."

The lad flushed up, and, going to the window, looked out for a few moments on the green, flickering, sun-lashed garden. "I owe a great deal to Harry, Basil," he said, at last—"more than I owe to you. You only taught me to be vain."

"Well, I am punished for that, Dorian—or shall be some day."

"I don't know what you mean, Basil," he exclaimed, turning round. "I don't know what you want. What do you want?"

"I want the Dorian Gray I used to paint," said the artist, sadly.

"Basil," said the lad, going over to him, and putting his hand on his shoulder, "you have come too late. Yesterday when I heard that Sibyl Vane had killed herself——"

"Killed herself! Good heavens! is there no doubt about that?" cried Hallward, looking up at him with an expression of horror.

"My dear Basil! Surely you don't think it was a vulgar accident? Of course she killed herself."

The elder man buried his face in his hands. "How fearful," he muttered, and a shudder ran through him.

"No," said Dorian Gray, "there is nothing fearful about it. It is one of the great romantic tragedies of the age. As a rule, people who act lead the most commonplace lives. They are good husbands, or faithful wives, or something tedious. You know what I mean—middle-class virtue, and all that kind of thing. How different Sibyl was! She lived her finest tragedy. She was always a heroine. The last night she played—the night you saw her—she acted badly because she had known the reality of love. When she knew its unreality, she died, as Juliet might have died. She passed again into the sphere of art. There is something of the martyr about her. Her death has all the pathetic uselessness of martyrdom, all its wasted beauty. But, as I was saying, you must not think I have not suffered. If you had come in yesterday at a particular moment—about half-past five, perhaps, or a quarter of six—you would have found me in tears. Even Harry, who was here, who brought me the news, in fact, had no idea what I was going through. I suffered immensely. Then it passed away. I cannot repeat an emotion. No one can, except sentimentalists. And you are awfully unjust, Basil. You come down here to console me. That is charming of you. You find me consoled, and you are furious. How like a sympathetic person! You remind me of a story Harry told me about a certain philanthropist who spent twenty years of his life in trying to get some grievance redressed, or some unjust law altered—I forget exactly what it was. Finally he succeeded, and nothing could exceed his disappointment. He had absolutely nothing to do, almost died of *ennui*, and became a confirmed misanthrope. And besides, my dear old Basil, if you really want to console me, teach me rather to forget what has happened, or to see it from a proper artistic point of view. Was it not Gautier who used to write about *la consolation des arts?* I remember picking up a little vellum-covered book in your studio one day and chancing on that delightful phrase. Well, I am not like that young man you told me of when we were down at Marlow together, the young man who used to say that yellow satin could console one for all the miseries of life. I love beautiful things that one can touch and handle. Old brocades, green bronzes, lacquer-work, carved ivories, exquisite surroundings, luxury, pomp, there is much to be got from all these. But the artistic temperament that they create, or at any rate reveal, is still more to me. To become the spectator of one's own life, as Harry says, is to escape the suffering of life. I know you are surprised at my talking to you like this. You have not realized how I have developed. I was a schoolboy when you knew me. I am a man now. I have new passions, new thoughts, new ideas. I am different, but you must not like me less. I am changed, but you must always be my friend. Of course I am very fond of Harry. But I know that you are better than he is. You are not stronger—you are too much afraid of life—but you are better. And how happy we used to be together! Don't leave me, Basil, and don't quarrel with me. I am what I am. There is nothing more to be said."

The painter felt strangely moved. The lad was infinitely dear to him, and his personality had been the great turning-point in his art. He could not bear the idea of reproaching him any more. After all, his indifference was probably merely a mood that would pass away. There was so much in him that was good, so much in him that was noble.

"Well, Dorian," he said, at length, with a sad smile, "I won't speak to you again about this horrible thing, after to-day. I only trust your name won't be mentioned in connection with it. The inquest is to take place this afternoon. Have they summoned you?"

Dorian shook his head, and a look of annoyance passed over his face at the mention of the word "inquest." There was something so crude and vulgar about everything of the kind. "They don't know my name," he answered.

"But surely she did?"

"Only my Christian name, and that I am quite sure she never mentioned to any one. She told me once that they were all rather curious to learn who I was, and that she invariably told them my name was Prince Charming. It was pretty of her. You must do me a drawing of Sibyl, Basil. I should like to have something more of her than the memory of a few kisses and some broken pathetic words."

"I will try and do something, Dorian, if it would please you. But you must come and sit to me yourself again. I can't get on without you."

"I can never sit to you again, Basil. It is impossible!" he exclaimed, starting back.

The painter stared at him. "My dear boy, what nonsense!" he cried. "Do you mean to say you don't like what I did of you? Where is it? Why have you pulled the screen in front of it? Let me look at it. It is the best thing I have ever done. Do take the screen away, Dorian. It is simply disgraceful of your servant hiding my work like that. I felt the room looked different as I came in."

"My servant has nothing to do with it, Basil. You don't imagine I let him arrange my room for me? He settles my flowers for me sometimes—that is all. No; I did it myself. The light was too strong on the portrait."

"Too strong! Surely not, my dear fellow? It is an admirable place for it. Let me see it." And Hallward walked towards the corner of the room.

A cry of terror broke from Dorian Gray's lips, and he rushed between the painter and the screen. "Basil," he said, looking very pale, "you must not look at it. I don't wish you to."

"Not look at my own work! you are not serious. Why shouldn't I look at it?" exclaimed Hallward, laughing.

"If you try to look at it, Basil, on my word of honour I will never speak to you again as long as I live. I am quite serious. I don't offer any explanation, and you are not to ask for any. But, remember, if you touch this screen, everything is over between us."

Hallward was thunderstruck. He looked at Dorian Gray in absolute amazement. He had never seen him like this before. The lad was actually pallid with rage. His hands were clenched, and the pupils of his eyes were like disks of blue fire. He was trembling all over.

"Dorian!"

"Don't speak!"

"But what is the matter? Of course I won't look at it if you don't want me to," he said, rather coldly, turning on his heel, and going over towards the window. "But, really, it seems rather absurd that I shouldn't see my own work, especially as I am going to exhibit it in Paris in the autumn. I shall probably have to give it another coat of varnish before that so I must see it some day, and why not to-day?"

"To exhibit it! You want to exhibit it?" exclaimed Dorian Gray, a strange sense of terror creeping over him. Was the world going to be shown his secret? Were people to gape at the mystery of his life? That was impossible. Something—he did not know what—had to be done at once.

"Yes; I don't suppose you will object to that. Georges Petit is going to collect all my best pictures for a special exhibition in the Rue de Sèze, which will open the first week in October. The portrait will only be away a month. I should think you could easily spare it for that time. In fact, you are sure to be out of town. And if you keep it always behind a screen, you can't care much about it."

Dorian Gray passed his hand over his forehead. There were beads of perspiration there. He felt that he was on the brink of a horrible danger. "You told me a month ago that you would never exhibit it," he cried. "Why have you changed your mind? You people who go in for being consistent have just as many moods as others have. The only difference is that your moods are rather meaningless. You can't have forgotten that you assured me most solemnly that nothing in the world would induce you to send it to any exhibition. You told Harry exactly the same thing." He stopped suddenly, and a gleam of light came into his eyes. He remembered that Lord Henry had said to him once, half seriously and half in jest, "If you want to have a strange quarter of an hour, get Basil to tell you why he won't exhibit your picture. He told me why he wouldn't, and it was a revelation to me." Yes, perhaps Basil, too, had his secret. He would ask him and try.

"Basil," he said, coming over quite close, and looking him straight in the face, "we have each of us a secret. Let me know yours, and I shall tell you mine. What was your reason for refusing to exhibit my picture?"

The painter shuddered in spite of himself. "Dorian, if I told you, you might like me less than you do, and you would certainly laugh at me. I could not bear your doing either of those two things. If you wish me never to look at your picture again, I am content. I have always you to look at. If you wish the best work I have ever done to be hidden from the world, I am satisfied. Your friendship is dearer to me than any fame or reputation."

"No, Basil, you must tell me," insisted Dorian Gray. "I think I have a right to know." His feeling of terror had passed away, and curiosity had taken its place. He was determined to find out Basil Hallward's mystery.

"Let us sit down, Dorian," said the painter, looking troubled. "Let us sit down. And just answer me one question. Have you noticed in the picture something curious?—something that probably at first did not strike you, but that revealed itself to you suddenly?"

"Basil!" cried the lad, clutching the arms of his chair with trembling hands, and gazing at him with wild, startled eyes.

"I see you did. Don't speak. Wait till you hear what I have to say. Dorian, from the moment I met you, your personality had the most extraordinary influence over me. I was dominated, soul, brain, and power by you. You became to me the visible incarnation of that unseen ideal whose memory haunts us artists like an exquisite dream. I worshipped you. I grew jealous of every one to whom you spoke. I wanted to have you all to myself. I was only happy when I was with you. When you were away from me you were still present in my art. . . . Of course I never let you know anything about this.

It would have been impossible. You would not have understood it. I hardly understood it myself. I only knew that I had seen perfection face to face, and that the world had become wonderful to my eyes—too wonderful, perhaps, for in such mad worships there is peril, the peril of losing them, no less than the peril of keeping them. . . . Weeks and weeks went on, and I grew more and more absorbed in you. Then came a new development. I had drawn you as Paris in dainty armour, and as Adonis with huntsman's cloak and polished boar-spear. Crowned with heavy lotus-blossoms you had sat on the prow of Adrian's barge, gazing across the green turbid Nile. You had leant over the still pool of some Greek woodland, and seen in the water's silent silver the marvel of your own face. And it had all been what art should be, unconscious, ideal, and remote. One day, a fatal day I sometimes think, I determined to paint a wonderful portrait of you as you actually are, not in the costume of dead ages, but in your own dress and in your own time. Whether it was the Realism of the method, or the mere wonder of your personality, thus directly presented to me without mist or veil, I cannot tell. But I know that as I worked at it, every flake and film of colour seemed to me to reveal my secret. I grew afraid that others would know of my idolatry. I felt, Dorian, that I had told too much, that I had put too much of myself into it. Then it was that I resolved never to allow the picture to be exhibited. You were a little annoyed; but then you did not realize all that it meant to me. Harry, to whom I talked about it, laughed at me. But I did not mind that. When the picture was finished, and I sat alone with it, I felt that I was right. . . . Well, after a few days the thing left my studio, and as soon as I had got rid of the intolerable fascination of its presence it seemed to me that I had been foolish in imagining that I had seen anything in it, more than that you were extremely good-looking and that I could paint. Even now I cannot help feeling that it is a mistake to think that the passion one feels in creation is ever really shown in the work one creates. Art is always more abstract than we fancy. Form and colour tell us of form and colour—that is all. It often seems to me that art conceals the artist far more completely than it ever reveals him. And so when I got this offer from Paris I determined to make your portrait the principal thing in my exhibition. It never occurred to me that you would refuse. I see now that you were right. The picture cannot be shown. You must not be angry with me, Dorian, for what I have told you. As I said to Harry, once, you are made to be worshipped."

Dorian Gray drew a long breath. The colour came back to his cheeks, and a smile played about his lips. The peril was over. He was safe for the time. Yet he could not help feeling infinite pity for the painter who had just made this strange confession to him, and wondered if he himself would ever be so dominated by the personality of a friend. Lord Henry had the charm of being very dangerous. But that was all. He was too clever and too cynical to be really fond of. Would there ever be some one who would fill him with a strange idolatry? Was that one of the things that life had in store?

"It is extraordinary to me, Dorian," said Hallward, "that you should have seen this in the portrait. Did you really see it?"

"I saw something in it," he answered, "something that seemed to me very curious."

"Well, you don't mind my looking at the thing now?"

Dorian shook his head. "You must not ask me that, Basil. I could not possibly let you stand in front of that picture."

"You will some day, surely?"

"Never."

"Well, perhaps you are right. And now good-bye, Dorian. You have been the one person in my life who has really influenced my art. Whatever I have done that is good, I owe to you. Ah! you don't know what it cost me to tell you all that I have told you."

"My dear Basil," said Dorian, "what have you told me? Simply that you felt that you admired me too much. That is not even a compliment."

"It was not intended as a compliment. It was a confession. Now that I have made it, something seems to have gone out of me. Perhaps one should never put one's worship into words."

"It was a very disappointing confession."

"Why, what did you expect, Dorian? You didn't see anything else in the picture, did you? There was nothing else to see?"

"No; there was nothing else to see. Why do you ask? But you mustn't talk about worship. It is foolish. You and I are friends, Basil, and we must always remain so."

"You have got Harry," said the painter, sadly.

"Oh, Harry!" cried the lad, with a ripple of laughter. "Harry spends his days in saying what is incredible, and his evenings in doing what is improbable. Just the sort of life I would like to lead. But still I don't think I would go to Harry if I were in trouble. I would sooner go to you, Basil."

"You will sit to me again?"

"Impossible!"

"You spoil my life as an artist by refusing, Dorian. No man came across two ideal things. Few come across one."

"I can't explain it to you, Basil, but I must never sit to you again. There is something fatal about a portrait. It has a life of its own. I will come and have tea with you. That will be just as pleasant."

"Pleasanter for you, I am afraid," murmured Hallward, regretfully. "And now good-bye. I am sorry you won't let me look at the picture once again. But that can't be helped. I quite understand what you feel about it."

As he left the room, Dorian Gray smiled to himself. Poor Basil! how little he knew of the true reason! And how strange it was that, instead of having been forced to reveal his own secret, he had succeeded, almost by chance, in wrestling a secret from his friend! How much that strange confession explained to him! The painter's absurd fits of jealousy, his wild devotion, his extravagant panegyrics, his curious reticences—he understood them all now, and he felt sorry. There seemed to him to be something tragic in a friendship so coloured by romance.

He sighed, and touched the bell. The portrait must be hidden away at all costs. He could not run such a risk of discovery again. It had been mad of him to have allowed the thing to remain, even for an hour, in a room to which any of his friends had access.

Homogenic Love and Its Place in a Free Society

Edward Carpenter

I.

THIS BRIEF SKETCH may suffice to give the reader some idea of the place and position in the world of the particular sentiment which we are discussing; nor can it fail to impress him—if any reference is made to the authorities quoted—with a sense of the dignity and solidity of the sentiment, at any rate as handled by some of the world's greatest men. At the same time it will be sure to arouse further questions. It will be evident from the instances given—and there would be no object in ignoring this fact—that this kind of love, too, like others, has its physical side; and queries will naturally arise as to the exact place and purport of the physical in it.

This is a subject which we shall have occasion to consider more in detail in the second part of this paper; but here a few general remarks may be made. In the first place we may say that to all love and indeed to all human feeling there must necessarily be a physical side. The most delicate emotion which plays through the mind has, we cannot but perceive, its corresponding subtle change in the body, and the great passions are accompanied by wide-reaching disturbances and transformations of corporeal tissue and fluid. Who knows (it may be asked) how deeply the mother-love is intertwined with the growth of the lacteal vessels and the need of the suckled infant? or how intimately even the most abstract of desires—namely the religious—is rooted in the slow hidden metamorphosis by which a new creature is really and physically born within the old? Richard Wagner, in a pregnant little passage in his "Communication to my Friends," says that the essence of human love "is the longing for utmost physical reality, for fruition in an object which can be grasped by all the senses, held fast with all the force of actual being." And if this is a somewhat partial statement it yet puts into clear language one undoubted relation between the sensuous and the emotional in all love, and the sweet *excuse* which this relation may be said to provide for the existence of the actual world—namely that the latter is the means whereby we become conscious of our most intimate selves.[2]

But if this is true of love in general it must be true of the Homogenic Love; and we must not be surprised to find that in all times this attachment has had some degree of physical expression. The question however as to *what* degree of physical intimacy may be termed in such a case fitting and natural—though a question which is sure to arise—is one not easy to answer: more especially as in the common mind any intimacy of a bodily nature between two persons of the same sex is so often (in the case of males) set down as a sexual act of the crudest and grossest kind. Indeed the difficulty here is that the majority of people, being incapable perhaps of understanding the *inner* feeling of the homogenic attachment,[3] find it hard to imagine that the intimacy has any other object than the particular form of sensuality mentioned (i.e. the *Venus aversa,* which appears, be it said, to be rare in all the northern countries), or that people can be held together by any tie except the most sheerly material one—a view which of course turns the whole subject upside down, and gives rise to violent and no doubt very natural disapprobation; and to endless recriminations and confusion.

Into this mistake we need not fall. Without denying that sexual intimacies do exist; and while freely admitting that, in great cities, there are to be found associated with this form of attachment prostitution and other evils comparable with the evils associated with the ordinary sex-attachment; we may yet say that it would be a great error to suppose that the homogenic love takes as a rule the extreme form vulgarly supposed; and that it would also be a great error to overlook the fact that in a large number of instances the relation is not distinctively

---

[2] See pamphlet, "Sex-Love," p. 7.

[3] As indeed the majority of people have a difficulty in appreciating the inner feeling of most love.

sexual at all, though it may be said to be physical in the sense of embrace and endearment. While it is not my object in this paper to condemn special acts or familiarities between lovers (since these things must no doubt be largely left to individual judgment, aided by whatever light Science or Physiology may in the future be able to throw upon the subject)—still I am anxious that it should be clearly understood that the glow of a really human and natural love between two persons of the same sex may be, and often is, felt without implying (as is so often assumed) mere depravity of character or conduct. No one can read the superb sonnets, already mentioned, of Shakespeare and Michelangelo without feeling, beneath the general mass of emotional utterance, the pulsation of a distinct bodily desire; and even Tennyson, somewhat tenuous and Broad-churchy as he is, is too great a master and too true a man not to acknowledge in his great comrade-poem "In Memoriam" (see Cantos XIII., XVIII., etc.) the passionateness of his attachment—for doing which indeed he was soundly rated by the *Times* at the time of its publication; yet it would be monstrous to suppose that these men, and others, because they were capable of this kind of feeling and willing to confess its sensuous side, were therefore particularly licentious.

With these few general remarks, and the conclusion, so far, that while the homogenic feeling undoubtedly demands *some* kind of physical expression, the question what degree of intimacy is in all cases fitting and natural may not be a very easy one to decide—we may pass on to consider what light is thrown on the whole subject by some recent scientific investigations.

That passionate attachment between two persons of the same sex is, as we have seen, a phenomenon widespread through the human race, and enduring in history, has been always more or less recognised; and once at least in history—in the Greek age—the passion rose into distinct consciousness, and justified, or even it might be said glorified, itself; but in later times—especially perhaps during the last century or two of European life—it has generally been treated by the accredited thinkers and writers as a thing to be passed over in silence, as associated with mere grossness and mental aberration, or as unworthy of serious attention.

In latest times however—that is, during the last thirty years or so—a group of scientific and capable men in Germany, France, and Italy—among whom are Dr. Albert Moll of Berlin; Krafft-Ebing, one of the leading medical authorities of Vienna, whose book on

"Sexual Psychopathy" has passed into its eighth edition; Dr. Paul Moreau ("des Aberrations du sens Génésique"); Cesare Lombroso, the author of various works on Anthropology; Tarnowski; Mantegazza; K. H. Ulrichs, and others—have made a special and more or less impartial study of this subject: with the result that a quite altered complexion has been given to it; it being indeed especially noticeable that the change of view among the scientists has gone on step by step with the accumulation of reliable information, and that it is most marked in the latest authors, such as Krafft-Ebing and Moll.

It is not possible here to go into anything like a detailed account of the works of these various authors, their theories, and the immense number of interesting cases and observations which they have contributed; but some of the general conclusions which flow from their researches may be pointed out. In the first place their labors have established the fact, known hitherto only to individuals, that *sexual inversion*—that is the leaning of sexual desire to one of the same sex—is in a vast number of cases quite instinctive and congenital, mentally and physically, and therefore twined in the very roots of individual life and practically ineradicable. To Men or Women thus affected with an innate homosexual bias, Ulrichs gave the name of Urning,[4] since pretty widely accepted by scientists. Too much emphasis cannot be laid on the distinction between these born lovers of their own sex, and that class of persons, with whom they are so often confused, who out of mere carnal curiosity or extravagance of desire, or from the dearth of opportunities for a more normal satisfaction (as in schools, barracks, &c.) adopt some homosexual practices. In the case of these latter the attraction towards their own sex is merely superficial and temptational, so to speak, and is generally felt by those concerned to be in some degree morbid. In the case of the former it is, as said, so deeply rooted and twined with the mental and emotional life that the person concerned has difficulty in imagining himself affected otherwise than he is; and to him at least the homogenic love appears healthy and natural, and indeed necessary to the concretion of his individuality.

In the second place it has become clear that the number of individuals affected with 'sexual inversion' in some degree or other is very great—much greater than is generally supposed to be the case. It is however very difficult or perhaps impossible to arrive at satisfactory

[4] From Uranos—because the celestial love was the daughter of Uranos (see Plato's "Symposium," speech of Pausanias).

figures on the subject, for the simple reasons that the proportions vary so greatly among different peoples and even in different sections of society and in different localities, and because of course there are all possible grades of sexual inversion to deal with, from that in which the instinct is *quite exclusively* directed towards the same sex,[5] to the other extreme in which it is normally towards the opposite sex but capable occasionally and under exceptional attractions, of inversion towards its own—this last condition being probably among some peoples very widespread, if not universal.

In the third place, by the tabulation and comparison of a great number of cases and "confessions," it has become pretty well established that the individuals affected with inversion in marked degree do not after all differ from the rest of mankind, or womankind, in any other physical or mental particular which can be distinctly indicated.[6] No congenital association with any particular physical conformation or malformation has yet been discovered; nor with any distinct disease of body or mind. Nor does it appear that persons of this class are usually of a gross or specially low type, but if anything rather the opposite—being often of refined sensitive nature and including, as Krafft-Ebing points out ("Psychopathia Sexualis," seventh ed., p. 227) a great number "highly gifted in the fine arts, especially music and poetry," and, as Mantegazza says,[7] many persons of high literary and social distinction. It is true that Krafft-Ebing insists on the generally strong sexual equipment of this class of persons (among men), but he hastens to say that their emotional love is also "enthusiastic and exalted,"[8] and that, while bodily congress is desired, the special act with which they are vulgarly credited is in most cases repugnant to them.[9]

The only distinct characteristic which the scientific writers claim to have established is a marked tendency to nervous development in the subject, not infrequently associated with nervous maladies;

[5] With regard to the number of these *quite exclusive* homosexuals (supposably born so) estimates vary, from one man in every 50 to one in every 500. See Moll. "Conträre Sexual-empfinding," second edn., p. 75.

[6] Though there is no doubt a general *tendency* towards femininity of type in the male Urning, and towards masculinity in the female.

[7] "Gli amori degli uomini."

[8] "Psychopathia Sexualis," seventh ed., p. 227.

[9] Ibid: pp. 229 and 258.

but—as I shall presently have occasion to show—there is reason to think that the validity even of this characteristic has been exaggerated.

Taking the general case of men with a marked exclusive preference for their own sex, Krafft-Ebing says ("P.S." p. 256) "The sexual life of these Homosexuals is *mutatis mutandis* just the same as in the case of normal sex-love . . . The Urning loves, deifies his male beloved one, exactly as the woman-wooing man does *his* beloved. For him, he is capable of the greatest sacrifice, experiences the torments of unhappy, often unrequited, love, of faithlessness on his beloved's part, of jealousy, and so forth. His attention is enchained only by the male form . . . The sight of feminine charms is indifferent to him, if not repugnant." Then he goes on to say that many such men, notwithstanding their actual aversion to intercourse with the female, do ultimately marry—whether from ethical, as sometimes happens, or from social considerations. But very remarkable—as illustrating the depth and tenacity of the homogenic instinct[10]—and pathetic too, are the records that he gives of these cases; for in many of them a real friendship and regard between the married pair was still of no avail to overcome the distaste on the part of one to sexual intercourse with the other, or to prevent the experience of actual physical distress after such intercourse, or to check the continual flow of affection to some third person of the same sex; and thus unwillingly, so to speak, this bias remained a cause of suffering to the end.

This very brief summary of scientific conclusions, taken in conjunction with the fact (which we have already referred to) that the whole literature and life of the greatest people of antiquity—the Greeks of the Periclean age—was saturated with the passion of homogenic or comrade-love, must convince us that this passion cannot be lightly dismissed as of no account— must convince us that it has an important part to play in human affairs. On the one hand we have anathemas and execrations, on the other we have the sublime enthusiasm of a man like Plato—one of the leaders of the world's thought for all time—who puts, for example, into the mouth of Phaedrus (in the *Symposium*) such a passage as this[11]: "I know not any greater blessing to a young man beginning life than a virtuous lover, or to the lover than a beloved youth. For the principle which ought

[10] "How deep congenital sex-inversion roots may be gathered from the fact that the pleasure-dream of the male Urning has to do with male persons, and of the female with females." (Krafft-Ebing "P.S." seventh ed., p. 228).

[11] Jowett's "Plato" (second ed.) Vol. II. p. 30.

to be the guide of men who would nobly live—that principle, I say, neither kindred, nor honour, nor wealth, nor any other motive is able to implant so well as love. Of what am I speaking? Of the sense of honour and dishonour, without which neither states nor individuals ever do any good or great work. . . . For what lover would not choose rather to be seen of all mankind than by his beloved, either when abandoning his post or throwing away his arms? He would be ready to die a thousand deaths rather than endure this. Or who would desert his beloved or fail him in the hour of danger? The veriest coward would become an inspired hero, equal to the bravest, at such a time; love would inspire him. That courage which, as Homer says, the god breathes into the soul of heroes, love of his own nature inspires into the lover." Or again in the "Phaedrus" Plato makes Socrates say[12]:—"In like manner the followers of Apollo and of every other god, walking in the ways of their god, seek a love who is to be like their god, and when they have found him, they themselves imitate their god, and persuade their love to do the same, and bring him into harmony with the form and ways of the god as far as they can; for they have no feelings of envy or jealousy towards their beloved, but they do their utmost to create in him the greatest likeness of themselves and the god whom they honour. Thus fair and blissful to the beloved when he is taken, is the desire of the inspired lover, and the initiation of which I speak into the mysteries of true love, if their purpose is effected." And yet Plato throughout his discourses never suggests for a moment that the love of which he is speaking is any other than the homogenic passion, nor glosses over or conceals its strong physical substructure.

[12] Jowett, vol. II., p. 130.

II.

We have now I think said enough to show from the testimony of History, Literature, Art, and even of Modern Science, that the homogenic passion is capable of splendid developments; and that a love and capacity of love of so intimate penetrating and inspiring a kind— and which has played so important a part in the life-histories of some of the greatest races and individuals—is well worthy of respectful and thoughtful consideration. And I think it has become obvious that to cast a slur upon this kind of love because it may in cases lead to aberrations and extravagances would be a most irrational thing to do—since exactly the same charges, of possible aberration and extravagance, might be brought, and the same conclusion enforced, against the ordinary sex-love.

It is however so often charged against the sentiment in question that it is essentially unnatural and *morbid* in character, that it may be worth while, though we have already touched on this point, to consider it here at greater length. I therefore propose to devote a few more pages to the examination of the scientific position on this subject, and then to pass on to a consideration of the general place and purpose of the homogenic or comrade-love (its sanity being granted) in human character and social life.

It might be thought that the testimonies of History, Literature and Art, above referred to, would be quite sufficient of themselves to dispose of the charge of essential morbidity. But as mankind in general is not in the habit of taking bird's eye views of History and Literature, and as it finds it easy to assume that anything a little exceptional is also morbid, so it is not difficult to see how this charge (in countries where the sentiment *is* exceptional) has arisen and maintained itself. Science, of course, is nothing but common observation organised and systemised, and so we naturally find that with regard to this subject it started on its investigations from the same general assumptions that possessed the public mind. It may safely be said that until the phenomena of homogenic Love began to be calmly discussed by the few scientific men already mentioned, the subject had never since classical times been once fairly faced in the arena of literature or public discussion, and had as a rule been simply dismissed with opprobrious epithets well suited to give an easy victory to prejudice and ignorance. But the history of even these few years of scientific investigation bears with it a memorable lesson. For while at the outset it was easily assumed that the homogenic instinct was thoroughly morbid in itself, and probably always associated with distinct disease, either physical or mental, the progress of the inquiry has—as already pointed out—served more and more to dissipate this view; and it is noticeable that Krafft-Ebing and Moll—the latest of the purely scientific authorities—are the least disposed to insist upon the theory of morbidity. It is true that Krafft-Ebing clings to the opinion that there is generally some *neurosis,* or degeneration of a nerve-centre, or *inherited tendency in that direction,* associated with the instinct; see p. 190 (seventh ed.), also p. 227, where he speaks, rather vaguely, of "an hereditary neuropathic or psychopathic tendency"—*neuro(psycho)pathische Belastung*. But it is an obvious criticism on this that there are few people in modern life, perhaps none, who could be pronounced absolutely free from such a *Belastung!* And whether the Dorian Greeks or the Polynesian Islanders or the Kelts (spoken of by Aristotle, Pol. ii. 7) or the Normans or the Albanian mountaineers, or any of the other notably hardy races among whom the passion has been developed, were particularly troubled by nervous degeneration we may well doubt![13]

As to Moll, though he speaks[14] of the instinct as morbid (feeling perhaps in duty bound to do so), it is very noticeable that he abandons the ground of its association with other morbid symptoms—as this association, he says, is by no means always to be observed; and is fain to rest his judgment on the *dictum* that the mere failure of the sexual instinct to propagate the species is itself pathological—a *dictum* which in its turn obviously springs from that prejudgment of scientists that generation is the sole object of love,[15] and which if pressed would

[13] It is interesting, too, to find that Walt Whitman, who certainly had the homogenic instinct highly developed, was characterised by his doctor, W. B. Drinkard, as having "the most natural habits, bases, and organisation he had ever met with or ever seen" in any man. "*In re* Walt Whitman," p. 115.

[14] "Conträre Sexual-empfindung," second ed., p. 269.

[15] See "Sex-Love," p. 23.

involve the good doctor in awkward dilemmas, as for instance that every worker-bee is a pathological specimen.

With regard to the nerve-degeneration theory, while it may be allowed that sexual inversion is not uncommonly found in connection with the specially nervous temperament, it must be remembered that its occasional association with nervous troubles or disease is quite another matter; since such troubles ought perhaps to be looked upon as the *results* rather than the causes of the inversion. It is difficult of course for outsiders not personally experienced in the matter to realise the great strain and tension of nerves under which those persons grow up from boyhood to manhood—or from girl to womanhood—who find their deepest and strongest instincts under the ban of the society around them; who before they clearly understand the drift of their own natures discover that they are somehow cut off from the sympathy and understanding of those nearest to them; and who know that they can never give expression to their tenderest yearnings of affection without exposing themselves to the possible charge of actions stigmatised as odious crimes.[16] That such a strain, acting on one who is perhaps already of a nervous temperament, should tend to cause nervous prostration or even mental disturbance is of course obvious; and if such disturbances are really found to be commoner among homogenic lovers than among ordinary folk we have in these social causes probably a sufficient explanation of the fact.

Then again in this connection it must never be forgotten that the medico-scientific enquirer is bound on the whole to meet with those cases that *are* of a morbid character, rather than with those that are healthy in their manifestation, since indeed it is the former that he lays himself out for. And since the field of his research is usually a great modern city, there is little wonder if disease colours his conclusions. In the case of Dr. Moll, who carried out his researches largely under the guidance of the Berlin police (whose acquaintance with the subject would naturally be limited to its least satisfactory sides), the only marvel is that his verdict is so markedly favorable as it is. As Krafft-Ebing says in his own preface "It is the sad privilege

[16] "Though then before my own conscience I cannot reproach myself, and though I must certainly reject the judgment of the world about us, yet I suffer greatly. In very truth I have injured no one, and I hold my love in its nobler activity for just as holy as that of normally disposed men, but under the unhappy fate that allows us neither sufferance nor recognition I suffer often more than my life can bear."—(Extract from a letter given by Krafft-Ebing.)

of Medicine, and especially of Psychiatry, to look always on the reverse side of life, on the weakness and wretchedness of man."

Having regard then to the direction in which science has been steadily moving in this matter, it is not difficult to see that the epithet "morbid" will probably before long be abandoned as descriptive of the homogenic bias—that is, of the general sentiment of love towards a person of the same sex. That there are excesses of the passion—cases, as in ordinary sex-love, where mere physical desire becomes a mania—we may freely admit; but as it would be unfair to judge of the purity of marriage by the evidence of the Divorce courts, so it would be monstrous to measure the truth and beauty of the attachment in question by those instances which stand most prominently perhaps in the eye of the modern public; and after all deductions there remains, we contend, the vast body of cases in which the manifestation of the instinct has on the whole the character of normality and healthfulness—sufficiently so in fact to constitute this *a distinct variety of the sexual passion*. The question, of course, not being whether the instinct is *capable* of morbid and extravagant manifestation—for this can easily be proved of any instinct—but whether it is capable of a healthy and sane expression. And this, we think, it has abundantly shown itself to be.

Anyhow the work that Science has practically done has been to destroy the dogmatic attitude of the former current opinion from which itself started, and to leave the whole subject freed from a great deal of misunderstanding, and much more open than before. Its labors—and they have been valuable in this way—have been chiefly of a negative character. While unable on the one hand to characterise the physical attraction in question as definitely morbid or the result of morbid tendencies, it is unable on the other hand to say positively at present what physiological or other purpose is attained by the instinct.

This question of the physiological basis of the homogenic love—to which we have more than once alluded—is a very important one; and it seems a strange oversight on the part of Science that it has hitherto taken so little notice of it. The desire for corporeal intimacy of some kind between persons of the same sex existing as it does in such force and so widely over the face of the earth, it would seem almost certain that there must be some physiological basis for the desire: but until we know more than we do at present as to what this basis may be, we are necessarily unable to understand the desire itself as well as we might wish. It may be hoped that this is a point to which attention will be given in the future. Meanwhile, though the problem is a complex one, it may not be amiss here to venture a suggestion or two.

In the first place it may be suggested that an important part of *all* love-union, mental or physical, is its influence personally on those concerned. This influence is, of course, subtle and hard to define; and one can hardly be surprised that Science, assuming hitherto in its consideration of ordinary sexual relations that the mutual actions and reactions were directed solely to the purpose of generation and the propagation of the species, has almost quite neglected the question of the direct influences on the lovers themselves. Yet everyone is sensible practically that there is much more in an intimacy with another person than the question of children alone; that even setting aside the effects of actual sex-intercourse there are subtle elements passing from one to another which are indispensable to personal well-being, and which make some such intimacy almost a necessary condition of health. It may be that there are some persons for whom these necessary reactions can only come from one of the same sex. In fact it is obvious there are such persons. "Successful love," says Moll (p. 125) "exercises a helpful influence on the Urning. His mental and bodily condition improves, and capacity of work increases—just as it often happens in the case of a normal youth with *his* love." And further on (p. 173) in a letter from a man of this kind occur these words: "The passion is I suppose so powerful, just because one looks for everything in the loved man—Love, Friendship, Ideal, and Sense-satisfaction. . . . As it is at present I suffer the agonies of a deep unresponded passion, which wake me like a nightmare from sleep. And I am conscious of physical pain in the region of the heart." In such cases the love, in some degree physically expressed, of another person of the same sex, is clearly as much a necessity and a condition of healthy life and activity, as in more ordinary cases is the love of a person of the opposite sex.

It has probably been the arbitrary limitation of the function of love to child-breeding which has (unconsciously) influenced the popular mind against the form of love which we are considering. That this kind of union was not concerned with the propagation of the race was in itself enough to make people look askance at it; that any kind of love-union could exist in which the sex-act might possibly *not* be the main object was an incredible proposition. And, in enforcing this view, no doubt the Hebraic and Christian tradition has exercised a powerful influence—dating, as it almost certainly does, from far-back times when the multiplication of the tribe was one of the very first duties of its members, and one of the first necessities of corporate life; though nowadays when the need has swung round all the other way it is not unreasonable to suppose that a similar revolution will take place in people's views of the place and purpose of the non-child-bearing love. We find in some quarters that even the most naive attachments between youths are stigmatised as "unnatural" (though, inconsistently enough, not those between girls)—and this can only well be from an assumption that all familiarities are meant by Nature to lead up to generation and race-propagation. Yet no one—if fairly confronted with the question—would seriously maintain that the mutual stimulus, physical mental and moral, which flows from embrace and endearment is nothing, and that because these things do not lead to actual race propagation therefore they must be discountenanced. If so, must even the loving association between man and wife, more than necessary for the breeding of children, or after the period of fertility has passed, be also discountenanced? Such questions might be multiplied indefinitely. They only serve to show how very crude as yet are all our theories on these subjects, and how necessary it is in the absence of more certain knowledge to suspend our judgment.[17]

Summarizing then some of our conclusions on this rather difficult question we may say that the homogenic love, as a distinct variety of the sex-passion, is in the main subject to the same laws as the ordinary love; that it probably demands and requires some amount of physical intimacy; that a wise humanity will quite recognise this; but that the degree of intimacy, in default of more certain physiological knowledge than we have, is a matter which can only be left to the good sense and feeling of those concerned; and that while we do not deny for a moment that excesses of physical appetite exist, these form no more reason for tabooing all expression of the sentiment than they do in the case of the more normal love. We may also say that if on the side of science much is obscure, there is no obscurity in the principles of healthy morality involved; that there is no exception here to the law that sensuality apart from love is degrading and something less than human; or to the law that love—true love—seeks nothing which is not consistent with the welfare of the loved one; and that here too the principle of Transmutation applies[18]—the principle that Desire in man has its physical emotional and spiritual sides, and that when its outlet is checked along one channel, it will, within limits, tend to flow with more vehemence along the other channels—and that

[17] "The truth is that we can no more explain the inverted sex-feeling than we can the normal impulse; all the attempts at explanation of these things, and of Love, are defective." (Moll, second ed. p. 253.)

[18] See "Sex-Love," p. 8.

reasonable beings, perceiving this, will (again within limits) check the sensual and tend to throw the centre of their love-attraction upwards.

Probably in this, as in all love, it will be felt in the end by those who devote themselves to each other and to the truth, to be wisest to concentrate on the *real thing,* on the enduring deep affection which is the real satisfaction and outcome of the relation, and which like a young sapling they would tend with loving care till it grows into a mighty tree which the storms of a thousand years cannot shake; and those who do so heartily and truly can leave the physical to take care of itself. This indeed is perhaps the only satisfactory touchstone of the rightness and fitness of human relations generally, in sexual matters. People, not unnaturally, seek for an absolute rule in such matters, and a *fixed* line between the right and the wrong; but may we not say that there is no rule except that of Love—Love making use, of course, of whatever certain knowledge Science may from time to time be able to provide?

And speaking of the law of Transmutation and its importance, it is clear, I think, that in the homosexual love—whether between man and man or between woman and woman—the physical side, from the very nature of the case, can never find expression quite so freely and perfectly as in the ordinary heterosexual love; and therefore that there is a 'natural' tendency for the former love to run rather more along emotional channels.[19] And this no doubt throws light on the fact that love of the homogenic type has inspired such a vast amount of heroism and romance—and is indeed only paralleled in this respect (as J. Addington Symonds has pointed out in his paper on Dantesque and Platonic ideals of Love)[20] by the loves of Chivalry, which of course owing to their special character, were subject to a similar transmutation.

It is well-known that Plato in many passages in his dialogues gives expression to the opinion that the love which at that time was common among the Greek youths had, in its best form, a special function in educational social and heroic work. I have already quoted a passage from the "Symposium," in which Phaedrus speaks of the inspiration which this love provides towards an honorable and heroic life. Pausanias in the same dialogue says[21]: "In Ionia and other places, and generally in countries which are subject to the barbarians, the custom is held to be dishonorable; loves of youths share the evil repute of philosophy and gymnastics *because they are inimical to tyranny,* for the

[19] See "Marriage," p. 7.

[20] See "In the Key of Blue" by J. A. Symonds. (Publ: by Elkin Matthews, 1893.)

[21] Jowett's "Plato," second ed. vol. ii. p. 33.

interests of rulers require that their subjects should be poor in spirit, and that there should be no strong bond of friendship or society between them—which love above all other motives, is likely to inspire, as our Athenian tyrants learned by experience." This is a pretty strong statement of the political significance of this kind of love.

Richard Wagner in his pamphlet "The Art-work of the Future"[22] has some interesting passages to the same effect—showing how the conception of the beauty of manhood became the formative influence of the Spartan State. He says:—"This beauteous naked man is the kernel of all Spartanhood; from genuine delight in the beauty of the most perfect human body—that of the male—arose that spirit of comrade-ship which pervades and shapes the whole economy of the Spartan State. This love of man to man, in its primitive purity, proclaims itself as the noblest and least selfish utterance of man's sense of beauty, for it teaches man to sink and merge his entire self in the object of his affection"; and again:—"The higher element of that love of man to man consisted even in this: that it excluded the motive of egoistic[23] physicalism. Nevertheless it not only included a purely spiritual bond of friendship, but this spiritual friendship was the blossom and the crown of the physical friendship. The latter sprang directly from delight in the beauty, aye in the material bodily beauty of the beloved comrade; yet this delight was no egoistic yearning, but a thorough stepping out of self into unreserved sympathy with the comrade's joy in himself; involuntarily betrayed by his life-glad beauty-prompted bearing. This love, which had its basis in the noblest pleasures of both eye and soul—not like our modern postal correspondence of sober friendship, half businesslike, half sentimental—was the Spartan's only tutoress of youth, the never-ageing instructress alike of boy and man, the ordainer of common feasts and valiant enterprises; nay the inspiring helpmeet on the battle-field. For this it was that knit the fellowship of love into battalions of war, and fore-wrote the tactics of death-daring, in rescue of the imperilled or vengeance for the slaughtered comrade, by the infrangible law of the soul's most natural necessity."

The last sentence in this quotation is well illustrated by a passage from a "privately printed" pamphlet entitled *A Problem in Greek Ethics,* in which the author endeavors to reconstruct as it were the genesis of comrade-love among the Dorians in early Greek times. Thus:—"Without sufficiency of women, without the sanctities of established domestic life, inspired by the memory of Achilles and

[22] Prose-works of Richard Wagner, translated by W. A. Ellis.

[23] The emphasis is on the word *egoistic.*

venerating their ancestor Herakles,[24] the Dorian warriors had special opportunity for elevating comradeship to the rank of an enthusiasm. The incidents of emigration into a distant country—perils of the sea, passages of rivers and mountains, assaults of fortresses and cities, landings on a hostile shore, night vigils by the side of blazing beacons, foragings for food, picquet service in the front of watchful foes—involved adventures capable of shedding the lustre of romance on friendship. These circumstances, by bringing the virtues of sympathy with the weak, tenderness for the beautiful, protection for the young, together with corresponding qualities of gratitude, self-devotion, and admiring attachment into play, may have tended to cement unions between man and man no less firm than that of marriage. On such connections a wise captain would have relied for giving strength to his battalions, and for keeping alive the flames of enterprise and daring." The author then goes on to suggest that though in such relations as those indicated the physical probably had its share, yet it did not at that time overbalance the emotional and spiritual elements, or lead to the corruption and effeminacy of a later age.

At Sparta the lover was called *Eispnêlos,* the inspirer, and the younger beloved *Aïtes,* the hearer. This alone would show the partly educational aspects in which comradeship was conceived; and a hundred passages from classic literature might be quoted to prove how deeply it had entered into the Greek mind that this love was the cradle of social chivalry and heroic life. Finally it seems to have been Plato's favorite doctrine that the relation if properly conducted led up to the disclosure of true philosophy in the mind, to the divine vision or mania, and to the remembrance or rekindling within the soul of all the forms of celestial beauty. He speaks of this kind of love as causing a "generation in the beautiful"[25] within the souls of the lovers. The image of the beloved one passing into the mind of the lover and upward through its deepest recesses reaches and unites itself to the essential forms of divine beauty there long hidden—the originals as it were of all creation—and stirring them to life excites a kind of generative descent of noble thoughts and impulses, which thenceforward modify the whole cast of thought and life of the one so affected.

---

[24] Whose tomb on account of his attachment to Iolaus was a place where Comrades swore troth to each other. (Plutarch on *Love,* section xvii.)

[25] "Symposium": Speech of Socrates.